I0520360

I Am The Streets

Book Two

T.L. Joy

Copyright © 2015 T.L. Joy

www.mahoganypublications.com

Table of Contents

Chapter One

Na'Tiva

"You can't just be sittin' here moping around. I know what happened to you was fucked up, but, bitch, it's time to get that money!" my sister, 'Tya, gleamed as she walked into my bedroom.

Since coming home from the hospital, my routine had consisted of physical therapy and sitting in my bedroom, isolated from the world. I didn't want to see nobody, and I for damn sure didn't want these bitches out here in Akron to see me like this. All the shit that I used to talk, all the times I strutted around on my high horse like I was the top-notch bitch, and here I was, finally getting my taste of karma.

It had been months since everything I had once had in my life was taken from me. I had nothing left to my name, and no love in my heart. Yeah, I wanted to find Brandon and get my revenge, but I knew that the process of doing that was not going to be easy.

"How are we going to get this money, 'Tya?" I finally asked.

"I know you've been out the loop with the street life since you left Akron years ago," Na'Tya began as she sat down on my bed, "but the owner of the strip club that I used to work for got murked around the time of your accident. Since then, the people who took over his club fucked up big time and got shut down. Some of the girls I know are working at theses cheap-ass clubs, but it's hard out here. I know they ain't making the money like they used to," she explained.

"So what are you tryin' to do?" I interjected.

"Look, I got some bread stacked up and I got whole lot of connections. I found this nice little spot to open up a bomb-ass strip club, but I need help. I'm not all business smart like you. I can be the face and get people up in the club, but all that legal back end shit, I don't know nothin' about. So how about you be my partner and handle all the back end shit for me?" she suggested, causing me to contemplate for a moment. This wasn't my ideal career choice, but at this point I needed money in order to get surgery for my face, and I was willing to do whatever I had to do...legally or illegally.

"Ok," I nodded. "I'm in."

"Good." She smiled. "I promise you, 'Tiva, we are going to make so much money it's gonna be crazy."

"That's wassup." I smiled in return. Making money was the first step of my plan.

Na'Tya

Everything was in full effect. Now that Big Buck was gone, my opportunity was wide open. Out of all the strip joints, Buck's old club was the largest club in the city and had the best clientele. Since his club was shut down, there was a huge need that had to be filled, and I was determined to be the one to take over the game.

After sitting in 'Tiva's bedroom discussing my plans for our club, she decided to type up our business plan and financial projections while I headed out to handle some business. I was glad that Na'Tiva was on board with opening up a strip club with me, but there was another aspect of business that needed to be taken care of. The one area that she knew nothing about and that I knew all too well.

"Did you find some good potential clients?" I asked as I sat down on the loveseat in our designated hotel suite.

"Yes...I sure did." Travis smiled, handing me a glass of Chardonnay. "Some of Buck's old clients talked to one of my associates, complaining that they can no longer get their desired services or in contact with their favorite girls," he continued as he sat down next to me.

"Oh really?" I raised an eyebrow.

"Yes. They loved the Fab Five and would like to work with them again. Are you able to get in contact with them?" Travis asked.

"Yeah, I can hit them bitches up. I heard they are stripping at a low-budget club. I know they are hurting for more money," I answered, thinking of ways to lure them in to work for me.

"Good. I have even better clientele, some in other countries that are willing to pay top dollar for services. But you are going to need more than five girls," he suggested firmly.

"I can get more than ten girls on my team, that's easy," I bragged, before downing my drink. Problem was, it wasn't going to be that easy, but I'd find a way.

"How soon can you do that? We can get this business up off the ground faster than opening up your strip club. Then that's more money for you," Travis explained.

"Hmm, I like the sound of that."

"Yeah. So we need to make that happen ASAP," he said.

"I will. Trust me," I replied, leaning back in the seat.

"Now enough of this business talk.... Time for your ass to get naked." Travis licked his lips as he eyed me up and down.

"Mmm, you ain't said nothing but a word." I smiled before standing before him and slipping out of my sundress, ready to embark on some sexual healing.

~ ~ ~

I spent two weeks after meeting with Travis recruiting some strippers to be on my team. Not for dancing, but to be an escort. I wanted to keep these girls separate. Unlike Buck, I wanted them to be full-time escorts and not just my favored strippers at the club. The more girls that were able to work full time, the more clients we could serve, and the more money me and Travis would make. Getting the girls on board to be on my "elite team" took some time, but once I told them that they would make more money than stripping, they were all in. We would provide them security, be discreet, and they could still have the lavish life without being known for stripping at the club. Once I got ten girls on the team, I focused my time on getting the club set up and getting old and new strippers on board. The first person I hit up was of course my girl Honey.

As we sat in her living room having a glass of Moscato, I began to talk business with her.

"You're trying to do what?" she laughed.

"I'm opening up a strip club," I repeated.

"Foreal? How you gonna do that?" Honey asked.

"I got connections girl!" I smiled before taking a sip of my drink.

"Yeah, aiight. I see you out here tryin' to get it," she nodded.

"Hell mothafuckin' yeah. But you know I can't leave my girl high 'n' dry. I know you barely makin' shit at them other clubs, so you should come be at my spot. My shit is about to be bigger than Bucks!" I suggested.

"Hmm." She twisted her mouth as she contemplated. I wasn't sure why it was taking her so long to just say yes. I mean, what other options did she have? And I know her ass didn't think she was about to get a percentage of this business. Her ass wasn't business smart at all.

"Aiight girl, I'm wit' it!" She smiled. I let out a sigh of relief.

"That's what I'm talkin' about bitch! We about to make this money," I gloated.

Now that I had Honey on my team, I knew that it would be easy to get the other girls to work for me. Honey was known to talk and tell everything to everybody. It would only be a matter of time before half of the strippers in this city would come to me personally, damn near begging to work for a bitch. A smile covered my face after I finished my drink. *Flawless Entertainment was about to blow up!*

Chapter Two

Na'Tya

Six months later

Meek Mill's "Check" blasted throughout my strip club as I sashayed through the crowded club, feeling like the boss bitch of the year. Money was flying from every direction as Honey and my girl Diva was upside down on the pole, giving a hell of a performance tonight. All the niggas with deep pockets were in full attendance, those ranging from NBA ballers to drug lords. As long as they was spendin' they money at the club, I didn't care what the fuck they did as their profession.

It had been six months since Flawless Entertainment opened up, and we were making hella' money. The escort business was even doing numbers as expected. We didn't just have the regular strippers and escorts from the local area, we had strippers from Detroit, Chicago, Houston, Miami, and even Brazilian and Columbian—immigrant women. Niggas loved having an exotic bitch in their presence, so that was our biggest advantage over the other strip clubs out here. We catered to every man's fantasy, and for that, we got paid!

All eyes were on me as I strutted past the bar dressed in a figure-hugging zippered black Givenchy dress that showed off my curves and my matching black Gladiator heels.

"Wassup Diamond D?" a tall, dark, and dreadlocked NFL player greeted me as I was walking past. Gently grabbing my hand, Adarius Williams stopped me so that I stood in front of his tall 6'3" frame.

I flashed him a Colgate smile in return. "Hello, Mr. Williams. Are you havin' a good time out here tonight?" I said, still remaining professional.

"Hell yeah! It's live up in here." He smiled.

"Good... Hey Lamar, get Mr. Williams a bottle of Rose on the house," I yelled out to the bartender.

"Yes boss," my bartender complied.

"Damn. Thanks ma'." Adarius said, looking fully impressed.

"No problem. You know I got to take care of my old clients." I winked before walking off. Adarius used to be one of my top clients when I worked for Buck. I know that he'll always remember me as Diamond Dior, but as of tonight, he got to see how much I changed since our last encounter. I was no longer an escort or a stripper, I was a business woman.

Finally making my way to the office upstairs, I walked in only to see my sister, 'Tiva, sitting at her desk with her eyes glued to the computer screen.

"The club is live as hell downstairs, and you're really sitting here on the computer?" I asked as I approached her.

"Look, I'm dealing with the numbers for this month. Someone gotta' balance the books," 'Tiva replied.

"Bitch, you know we can hire an accountant. But I feel you. If I had to trust anybody with our money, I can only trust yo' ass," I chuckled.

"Exactly." She smiled.

T.L. Joy

"But c'mon, 'Tiva, yo' ass has never went out on the floor since we opened the club. I know you concerned about your face and what people will think of it, but we know that you are stacking up yo' bread to get all the surgeries you need. You can't wait until your last surgery to come downstairs and see the club in action," I explained.

"No...I'm not going out there," she protested.

"C'mon, 'Tiva. For me?" I pleaded. "You don't have to go all the way to the stage or nothin'. We can just stand by the bottom step where you can see everyone. The niggas are going to be so into what the dancers are doing they won't even see us," I suggested.

Na'Tiva sat there and contemplated for a minute before hesitantly replying. "Fine," she sighed. "Only standing at the bottom step."

"That's what I'm talkin' about. You got to see how it looks when it's jammed packed," I gleamed in excitement as I hugged her. "Now let's go. You got to see Honey and Diva perform. They are out cold!" I smiled as I grabbed her hand, pulling her out of her seat and leading her out of the office. I knew she was nervous as hell, but she couldn't live like a hermit forever.

Na'Tiva

My breath quickened as I finally approached the bottom step, staring out into the club. There were so many faces that I felt my anxiety increase. I knew that they weren't staring at me, but it still felt like all eyes were on me. How could I have gone from being a beautiful, self-confident woman to a paranoid and self-conscious freak in a matter of a year?

I tried to distract myself by looking at the strippers entertaining us on the stage, but on the other side of the stage, I noticed a familiar face peering back at me from the front row of the crowd. The face of the man that I once knew caused fear to rip through my body. I instantly looked away. Maybe my eyes were playing tricks on me. I did a double take, but the man I thought I had seen was gone. *Maybe I'm trippin'.*

I looked over to Na'Tya, who seemed amused by how the club had turned out, but I couldn't stand being out here any longer.

"I'm going back upstairs 'Tya! This is too much..." I yelled out to her over the loud music.

"Huh?" she yelled back.

"Going upstairs," I said, pointing up to the office.

"Ok." She nodded her head before I made my way up the stairs.

Once I got into the office, I sat at my desk and pulled out my handheld mirror from my drawer. I took a good look at my face and felt disgusted. Ugly keloid scars covered my entire face, and my once smooth brown skin now looked hideous and discolored. I knew that as of now I was ugly on the outside, but I'd always known I was ugly on the inside. Especially after the fucked up shit that I'd done to people in my past.

Flashback

Before my life turned for the worst, I was a normal teenage girl out here in Akron. It was my senior year of high school and I had high hopes of graduating and going to college. I was still in my relationship with B-Moore and always had my best friend Danielle by my side. Life was good, until that one week of spring break came along and I caught wind of B-Moore cheating on me with some hating-ass cheerleader.

"What the fuck B?" I yelled as I walked into his bedroom.

"How the fuck could you cheat on me?" I yelled as I stationed myself in between him and his video game that he was occupied with.

"Cheat on you? 'Tiva yo' ass is trippin'." He raised his eyebrow.

"Hell no! Danielle saw you and Keisha come out the bathroom at Jenkin's party. Yo' ass was zippin' up yo' pants while she was fixing her skirt. Don't lie to me nigga," I spat.

"That's what the fuck Danielle said? You can't believe her lyin' ass. She hatin' on us 'Tiva. Don't you see that?" He raised his voice.

"Nah, don't call my girl a liar B. I'm done with yo' bullshit. It's over!" I said, walking away from his ass.

"Are you foreal?" he asked in disbelief.

"Hell yeah. Fuck you!" I yelled while heading out his room with him hot on my tail.

"You just gonna throw everything away over what some lyin' ass bitch said?" he yelled while I made my way outside his house.

"Don't talk shit about my friend!" I turned around and yelled back at him angrily.

"Whateva 'Tiva. You out here actin' stupid just like that hoe," he sneered.

"Fuck you!" was all I said before I marched off his porch and made my way down the block to my house. Hot tears stained my face as my blood boiled from anger. I couldn't believe how disrespectful his ass was, but that's ok, I was going to get the fuck outta Akron and meet a new nigga who was on a different level than his ass. Once I got to my house, I called up my girl Danielle to let her know what just happened.

"What!" she screeched over the phone. "I knew Brandon's bitch ass would deny what happened. And I can't believe he calling me a lyin' ass bitch! His momma was the lyin' bitch when she cheated on his daddy with my uncle...lil fuck nigga!" she continued ranting, causing me to let out a laugh.

"Yo' ass is crazy..." I chimed in as I laid on my bed staring out the window.

"Hell the fuck yeah! I'm not about to let some nigga disrespect my best friend like that. I should go to his house and whoop his ass! You are too pretty and smart to be cheated on. Especially with some raggedy ass bitch at that!" Danielle replied.

"You right girl," I nodded.

"Look. I know yo' ass is over there cryin' 'n' shit, but it's the start of our spring break and we need to be having some fun. Not moping around over a cheatin' ass nigga. Corey is havin' a party tonight, so I think we should go out and have some fun," she suggested.

"Hmm, I don't—" I began but was cut off.

"Naw bitch, yo' ass is coming. I'm on my way over there now. We are going to get cute as fuck and get loose tonight. See you in five," she interjected before hanging up on me.

Just like she said, Danielle arrived at my house within five minutes.

"Hey girl," she greeted, immediately hugging me as soon as I opened the door.

"Where's 'Tya's little ass at?" She asked as she stepped into the entryway and looked around.

"Girl, I don't even know. Probably out hangin' with Honey." I shrugged.

"Mmm, she gotta watch out for that girl. Honey is known to get into some mess," Danielle said, scrunching up her face in disgust.

"I bet..."

"Aww, you look so sad." Danielle hugged me again. "I know you loved him and all, but fuck that nigga girl. He wasn't shit anyway," she continued, making me laugh.

"That's better. Now c'mon and let's get ready for tonight." Danielle smiled as she grabbed my hand and led me upstairs to my bedroom, like this was her house.

That was one thing I loved about Danielle, even though she was crazy as all hell, she was always the one to cheer you up and be there for you no matter how bad it was. She was a real bitch and was all about loyalty. Something you don't find too often out here on these streets.

I sat on the bed and watched as Danielle released her long and wavy black hair out of her ponytail holder. "Girl I want to do something with my hair. You still got that flat iron?" she asked.

"All that pretty hair and you want to straighten it?" I raised my eyebrow.

"Bitch! You can have this shit. Sometimes I just want a different look ok? Don't judge me! You don't know my life!" she snapped.

"Whateva trick. Let me go get it. I think it's in 'Tya's room." I rolled my eyes as I hopped off my bed.

After retrieving the flat iron, I came back into the room to give it to Danielle. Not only did she have long wavy hair, but she had smooth dark skin, almond-shaped sienna brown eyes, perfect high cheekbones, and a coke bottle shape to match. You couldn't help but to hate on her beauty, but at the end of the day she was my best friend who had been by my side since elementary.

"Here you go," I said, handing it to her.

"Thanks girl. So uh, do you want to help me straighten this shit or what?" she laughed.

"Oh lawd!"

"Please. Then I can flat iron your hair and do your makeup..."

"Makeup? What the fuck I need makeup for?" I scrunched up my face.

"Look, everybody is about to be at this party tonight. Let's just try something new and have fun ok? We gotta get our grown and sexy on." She winked at me.

I let out a sigh as I plopped back onto the bed. "Aiight whateva'...this shit better be fun tonight."

"It will be, I promise," she reassured while flashing me her Colgate smile. Yet something in the pit of my stomach gave me a feeling that it was going to be anything but fun.

~~~

Music was blasting from the house that stood before us as soon as I hopped out of Danielle's Ford Taurus. People with red cups in their hands flooded from the front door of the house all the way out to the sidewalk. I could tell that this party was live. Pulling down my tight red dress over my thick thighs, I began to strut toward the front door with Danielle by my side. All eyes were on us as we were dressed in our tight, short dresses and heels.

"Damn ma...can I holla' at you for a minute?" A tall, light skin boy with green eyes asked as I walked past.

I looked at him and smiled, but before I could say anything Danielle grabbed me by my arm and damn near dragged me up the porch steps.

"C'mon girl. You can talk to him later," she yelled out.

"What the fuck was that about?" I questioned as we got close to the door.

"Girl, I got some people to meet. And after you meet them, I'm sure you won't want to fuck with his ass," she replied before we stepped into the hot and dimly-lit party.

"Pop Bottles" by Birdman and Lil Wayne blasted throughout the house as I followed Danielle toward the kitchen area. Girls were twerking like there was no tomorrow while niggas threw up cups and bottles in the air, getting hype off the song.

As soon as we walked into the kitchen, my eyes locked onto a familiar face. He was tall, standing about 6'2" with smooth brown skin, dark bedroom eyes, freshly cut taper fade, and was looking fresh as hell in the latest designer. I couldn't help but notice the distinct scar that fell from his right temple to underneath his cheekbone. Once his eyes locked with mine, he flashed me a smile, showing off his pearly whites. Damn, even with his imperfection, he still was fine as hell. He was surrounded by a slew of niggas that looked like they weren't the ones to be fucked with.

"Wassup fellas!" Danielle greeted.

"Hey sexy." Another tall and sexy brown skin guy from the crew walked up and hugged her.

"Wassup D. Who's ya' friend?" said the sexy man that I've been seeing around town.

"Oh, this my girl 'Tiva. Tiva, this is Reaper," Danielle introduced.

"The Reaper huh? Some type of name," I said sarcastically.

A smirk covered his face. "Just somethin' niggas on the streets call me."

"I see..." I chimed in.

"I'm sure you seen me around," he said with full confidence.

"Maybe." I shrugged, causing him to chuckle.

"I know you have. I'm well known out here ma'." He winked. "Let's cut the small talk. We got more than enough time to get to know each otha'. You want a drink?" he asked. Without hesitation, I nodded my head.

"What you drink?"

"Shit, whateva' you got for us!" Danielle chimed in, causing me to let out a laugh.

"Aiight...Aye J-dubb, go get these girls some of that Belvedere and cranberry we got," he commanded.

"Aiight boss," the short and stubby light skin man said before fixing us a drink.

Boss huh? I thought to myself. *This nigga must have pull to have people callin' him boss.* He was on a totally different caliber than what Brandon was on, who was clearly on that typical high school teenage shit. Reaper was on some real boss shit, and for that, I liked him even more.

"Here you go," J-dubb said, breaking my thoughts as he handed me and Danielle our red cups.

"Thanks," I simply stated before taking a sip of my drink. The strong vodka quickly filled my system and was strong enough to clear my damn nostrils. I was damn near tipsy just from half of my drink.

By the time I was on my second drink, we all moved to the upstairs bedroom that was dark and filled with strobe lights. Danielle sat on her niggas lap, taking a shotgun from him, while I sat next to Reaper with his arm around my waist. I'm usually not the type to be up under a nigga that I just met, but there was something about him that made me feel so safe and comfortable. That whole time, we sat and got to know each other.

I watched him as he began to spark a fat blunt as my favorite song, "House Party" by Meek Mill, blasted loudly throughout the house.

"You want some?" he asked after exhaling a thick cloud of smoke.

"Yeah..." I smiled.

"You don't seem like the type to spark up with yo' pretty ass," he chuckled.

"Pretty girls smoke too." I winked.

"Aiight." He nodded and smiled as he handed me the oversized blunt.

"I'm really feelin' you ma'," he said as I exhaled the smoke through my nose.

"Oh yeah?" I smirked.

"Yeah.... You need to stop fuckin' with those lame ass niggas and get with the winning team," he replied, making me laugh once again.

"So you the winning team?"

"You already know. I can get you anything you need and want. No problem ma'," he said, licking his luscious lips.

"Mmm, ok. We'll see about that." Just then, my phone rang and my mom's number flashed across the screen. Once I realized that it was close to 4 a.m., I knew why she was calling. I was way past my curfew of 2 a.m.

"Aye Danielle, we gotta go," I yelled out.

"Oh ok," she replied before hopping off her boo's lap and grabbing her things.

"Let me walk ya'll to the car," The Reaper insisted.

"Aiight." I smiled before we walked out of the bedroom and made our exit out of the house.

Once we got to our car, Reaper opened the door for me and helped me in. I couldn't help but notice one of his goons stood behind him as if he needed protection.

"So when am I goin' to see you again ma?" he asked.

"I don't know." I shrugged.

"You know...and when you do, give me a call," he said as he handed me piece of paper with his number on it.

"I'll think about it," I replied, playing hard to get. Yet that only made him laugh.

"Yeah, alright. I'll be expectin' that phone call ma'. Ya'll make it home safely," he said before taking one last look at me and walking off with his goon trailing closely behind him.

As soon as we pulled off, Danielle couldn't wait to start talkin' her shit.

"Bitch! I can't believe you had the mothafuckin' Reaper all in yo' face and talkin' that good shit too!" she gleamed.

"It's just a nigga." I rolled my eyes.

"Just a nigga?" she snapped. "Bitch, do you know who the fuck he is?"

"I guess not by how you acting," I answered.

"The Reaper and his crew runs the streets. Every nigga that works on the block works for the Reaper. I swear he got money out the fuckin' ass, and I ain't never seen him pressed for a bitch the way he was pressed for you tonight. Ever!" she exclaimed.

"Oh really?" My eyebrow raised out of curiosity. Hearing all of this peeked my interest.

"Yes really! These females out here stay flockin' for him, acting hella thirsty to just get a taste of that dick. They be dyin' to be his main chick. And here you are acting all hard to get? Girlllll! You betta' give that man a chance. Shit, he'll do more for you than B-Moore could ever do in his lifetime. Foreal," she explained as she sped down the highway.

"Damn..." was all I could say.

"Yes, that nigga is the truth. You'd be crazy to turn him down," she replied.

"Didn't you get rejected for that scholarship that you really needed anyway?" she asked, bringing up another one of my problems that had arrived last week.

"I'm not telling you to suck his dick for some paper or nothing, but I'm telling you that if you give him a chance and play the game right, he'll give you whatever you need for school. Shit, that nigga would probably pay yo' damn tuition if you was his main chick. If I were you, I'd be all over that shit," Danielle continued.

I never even thought about shit like that, but Danielle definitely had a point. "I hear you girl," I coined in.

"I hope so. Cause if you get with him, yo' life would be set. Fuck B-Moore and his wack shit. You too pretty to be with a broke nigga. You need you a boss," Danielle replied before pulling up to my house. "Just think about it girl," she continued.

"Aiight, I will. I'll see you tomorrow trick," I said as I grabbed my stuff and hopped out of her car.

"Aiight hoochie. See ya' tomorrow," Danielle replied before pulling out of the driveway and zooming down the street.

Even though Danielle and I saw things differently, I had to admit that she had a point about the Reaper. I've been struggling with Brandon for too long. I know people be saying broke love is the best love, but shit...in my world, that shit was wack. When a girl need money for school, and financial aid is on that bullshit, I need a nigga who is going to be able to invest in a bitch.

As I laid in my bed, replaying everything in my mind, I decided that I'm gonna do something different and give the sexy ass Reaper a chance. Shit, it couldn't hurt. At the end of the day, you only live once, so why not give that nigga a try? I mean, what's the worst that could happen?

~~~

After that night at the party, I finally decided to call the Reaper and give him a chance. Ever since then, my life changed rapidly. For the rest of my spring break, I spent every moment with him. Our connection was so strong, and on a whole different level than with B-Moore. We shared everything together. He even told me his government name, which was Jerrod, but he gained the name "the Reaper" due to his reputation of what he would do to niggas who would fuck with him or his money. Other girls would be scared by that fact, but not me.

Instead, I admired the fact that he was about his business and was not one to be fucked with...even though I would never see that side of him. Jerrod was lighthearted and loving towards me. He was wining and dining me and we hadn't even had sex yet. Everything was based off mental stimulation and our strong physical attraction to one another, and I loved every moment of it.

A month after spring break, I was officially his girl. He would take me on weekly shopping sprees, pay for me to get my nails and hair done weekly, and would even let me push one of his whips to school, since he didn't want his girl to be taking public transportation. He wasn't lying when he said that I needed to join the winning team, cause as soon as I gave him a chance, my life changed for the better.

A smile crept over my face as I walked into school looking cute as fuck in my tan leather jacket, light blue true religion jeans that hugged my curves perfectly, and my tan Manolo Blahnik Timbs, which were hot at that time. All eyes were on me as I walked down the hallway towards my locker.

"There go Reaper's girl," I heard one of the football players say to his friends who were posted up on their lockers close to mine.

"Foreal?" another player chimed in. "Damn, well I can see why. She is bad ass hell. I know she taken and all, but maybe she can have a friend," he continued.

"Nah man...you don't want to fuck with her cause the Reaper will leave yo' ass stinkin' in the streets. Just fall back on that," the tall player shut his friend down, causing me to laugh to myself. Just the fact that niggas knew who I was and that I wasn't the one to be fucked with made me feel like that bitch.

"So that's how you gonna do me 'Tiva?" Brandon yelled out as he approached me.

"What the fuck are you talkin' about?" My face scrunched up in confusion.

"You gonna just drop a nigga and get with someone else, that fuckin' fast though? And the Reaper at that?" he snapped.

"What the fuck ever Brandon. You're the one who cheated, so don't come at me like that. Shit, a real nigga was checkin' for a bitch and you just mad that I'm his and he treating me better than you ever could," I ranted, hitting him below the belt.

Brandon's face turned red from anger. "Fuck you Tiva," he snarled. "Since you think Reaper is a real nigga, then stay with that fuck nigga. Yo' ass don't know nothin' about the drug game, but you ova' here thinkin' you that bitch since you all up on his arm. But that's gonna change real quick when shit get real, and that nigga want you to do more than just look cute and suck his dick. Yo' ass will learn then and you gonna remember what the fuck I said to you..." Brandon went off, but I abruptly brushed him off.

"Shut the fuck up Brandon. I don't want to hear shit else you got to say," I shot back as I closed my locker and walked off. Brandon was just hating cause he lost me to a boss, something he could never be.

Once lunch time came, I sat at the table with Danielle and told her everything that was going on.

"Hell yeah. You know that nigga was hatin' hard," she laughed.

"Right! He was out there trippin'." I shook my head.

"Mmm, well fuck him and what he was talkin' about. You got too many good things happening right now to be worryin' about his drama and lies," Danielle said.

"You right." I smiled at the thought. My eighteenth birthday was this weekend, prom was next week, and graduation was at the end of this month. So I could care less about B-Moore and his shit.

"So you got any plans for this weekend?" Danielle asked, snapping me out of my thoughts.

"Well, Jerrod said that he had something special planned for me this weekend. I don't know what exactly it is, but knowing him, it gotta' be something big."

"Aww shit! It's going down!" Danielle exclaimed.

"Yes girl. If we go to a club or something, I'll keep you posted. You know I gotta have my girl come through and straight stunt." I smiled.

"Aiight girl. Just let me know and I'll be there."

"Of course," I gleamed. I couldn't wait for this weekend. Turning eighteen was one thing, but spending it with my sexy ass man was even better. Excitement surged through my body at the thought. I couldn't wait for this weekend.

~~~

Dressed in my royal blue high-low dress and my matching heels, I stood in front of the large bathroom in the executive suite of our five star hotel. After curling my long hair and adding the finishing touches to my light makeup, I was ready for the night that Jerrod had planned for me.

"You lookin' nice ma'," Jerrod said as he leaned against the bathroom doorway.

"Thanks babe." I turned around and smiled.

"Mmm, I might not even want yo' ass to leave this room tonight." He licked his lips as his eyes roamed my curves.

"Oh yeah? That might be an option," I said as I walked over to him and put my arms around his broad shoulders.

Wrapping his arms around my waist, Jerrod pulled me in closer and palmed my ass with his large hands. I stood up on my tippy toes to plant a kiss on his soft lips. He might be the cold hearted Reaper in the streets, but with me he was the loving

Jerrod who would do damn near anything to keep a smile on my face.

"You keep this up we really ain't leaving here," he joked as he lightly smacked my ass.

I giggled in response. "Nah...I gotta go out and enjoy my b-day first. Then whatever happens when we get back, is whatever happens."

He smiled. "Aiight...well let's go ma'. I got something nice planned for you tonight."

I couldn't help but smile in response as Jerrod took my hand and led me out of the hotel room.

Once we arrived at the club, we were immediately escorted up to the private V.I.P section upstairs. The whole upstairs section was all white with sleek white couches and was filled with

Reaper's people and my girl Danielle dressed in white.

"Happy Birthday bitch!" Danielle yelled out as she rushed over to me and hugged me.

"Time to turn the fuck up!" she continued as she grabbed my hand and led me to the dance floor area.

Trey Songz's "Say Aah" blasted throughout the club as we began dancing without a care in the world. The shot girls kept the bottles coming in rotation. Even though I wasn't old enough to legally drink, nobody said shit as I took Grey Goose to the head straight from the bottle. We were live as fuck up in the club, and I felt like the queen of the world as Jerrod wrapped his arms around me from the back and I grinded on his erect dick.

The liquor was getting to me, and the more I danced with Jerrod, the more I wanted his sexy ass. Moving off the dance floor, we made our way to a couch. As he began to spark a Cuban cigar, I sat on his lap and began to give him a lap dance to one of the freaky ass songs playing throughout the club.

"Mmm, I see you havin' a good time ma," he said.

"Hell yeah. Thanks to you babe!" I yelled over the music as I turned toward him and hugged him.

He licked his lips and flashed me that Colgate smile. "Good. I got something else for you ma'," he replied before signaling to one of his niggas to come here.

Without hesitation, J-dubb walked up to us with a Tiffany & Co. gift bag in his hand. Just the sight of that made me gleam in excitement.

"Are you fuckin' serious?" I screeched as J-dubb handed it to me.

"Open it." Jerrod nodded, and without a second thought, I opened up the bag only to see three boxes. *What the hell!*

I pulled out the first rectangular box, and as soon as I opened it, my eyes landed on a diamond-studded necklace.

"Custom made for my baby," he said proudly. "Check out the rest."

I pulled out the other two boxes and began to open them. One was a matching diamond-studded tennis bracelet and the other was matching diamond earrings.

"Damn...thank you babe!" was all I could say before I kissed him. My baby was making sure that a bitch was about to be laced. I never had someone buy me jewelry, and Tiffany's at that? I was seriously fuckin' with a boss, and just like Danielle said, I deserved to be with a nigga who would give me the world, not look at me when shit gets rough and say, "What you gon' do babe?" I'm so glad I got rid of Brandon and moved on to a real nigga!

We continued to turn up for the rest of the night at the club, and once the party was over, it was time to head back to the room and show Jerrod just how much I loved him.

As soon as we hit the bedroom we were on it, pulling each other's clothes off as we kissed and sucked on each other. Picking me up and putting my legs over his broad shoulders, his hands stayed planted on my ass while he backed me up onto the wall and ate my pussy just like that. My legs shook wildly as his tongue rapidly flicked over my clit until I couldn't hold it any longer and released my love into his mouth. In one fluid motion, he threw me onto the bed, got on top of me, and slid his thick ten inches inside of me, causing me to moan loudly. I tightly gripped the sheets as he pumped in and out of me in a fast pace, driving me insane. The way he was fuckin' me was like no other, and he made my body come alive. Over and over again, I continuously came on his dick as he hit my g-spot with each thrust. Although I hadn't had sex with many others, this was the best sex that I'd ever had.

After we both came in unison, I laid in his arms in pure bliss. At that moment I knew that I was never leaving his ass. This man was the one for me, despite his affiliations with the streets. I didn't care what anybody had to say about him, this was the man who I wanted to spend the rest of my life with. That night, I fell asleep in his arms, feeling safe and secure.

~~~

It seemed like everything moved fast pace after my birthday. My life was changing rapidly, but I was fortunate to have Jerrod by my side. Yet, a month after graduation was when shit changed in our relationship. I stood in front of the mailbox staring at the papers that were stationed in my hands.

"What the fuck!" I yelled out. All of the scholarships that I applied for weeks ago denied me because I had a 3.9 GPA instead of a perfect 4.0. This was straight bullshit. I wasn't cool with just going to Jerrod about my money woes too soon in our relationship, so I'd tried to find other alternatives. Unfortunately, they didn't pan out as I'd planned, so now it was time to take a piece of Danielle's advice and have that nigga help pay for my schooling. We'd been together for three months now, and our relationship had been off the chain since we'd been getting intimate almost every day, so I didn't see a reason for him to say no.

Folding up my rejection letters, I stomped back into the house and made my way up the stairs, practically pushing 'Tya out of my way.

"Damn, what is wrong with you?" she spat.

"Nothin'. Just leave me alone 'Tya," I groaned as I got closer to my bedroom.

"Whateva' 'Tiva. You been acting brand new since you got with the Reaper," 'Tya continued as she headed down the stairs, but I didn't have time to argue with her like I normally did. I had bigger fish to fry. Like getting 40,000 dollars for my first year of college.

I plopped onto my bed after grabbing my cell phone off the nightstand. It was now or never.

Dialing Jerrod's number, he answered on the first ring.

"What's up ma? Everything ok?"

"No. It's all bad. We need to talk," I sighed.

"Aiight, let me finish up this business and I'm on my way," he said before we hung up.

Within ten minutes, Jerrod's all-black Range Rover pulled up in front of my house. I hopped into the back seat with him as his driver began to pull off. Jerrod was never without at least one of his goons when we were out in public. Always paranoid that someone might shoot him while he was driving, Jerrod always had a driver, even though his car was bullet proof. I wasn't use to being with someone so paranoid of dying, but with his lifestyle I understood. When you're at the top, niggas will do anything to take your place, and Jerrod would be damned to let someone do that to him.

Once we pulled up to his mansion, we immediately went straight up into his master bedroom. I laid on his chest as I began to pour out my problems.

"Damn ma..." he began. "So you got into Spelman and you got denied from all those scholarships you applied for?"

"Yeah..." I sighed. "I don't know what the fuck I'm going to do babe. I need to go to school. I can't be like these other girls not doing shit, you know? But financial aid is on that bullshit cause when my mom was working she made too much money, even though she got laid off and can't help me out now. I don't know what I'm gonna do," I explained.

Anxiety crept over me as he was silent for a minute. *Damn, did I do the wrong thing by bringing this up to him?*

"I feel your situation, ma. That shit is fucked up. You got an opportunity to get out the hood and do better for yourself. Not too many niggas can do that. If I had an opportunity like that and were in yo' situation, I would want someone to look out for me. We all need somebody to be there for us in our time of need, and you not like these other girls out here. You are too smart to be out here strippin' and selling pussy for dollas. That's why I made you my girl," he explained, causing me to smile at his compliment.

"So for that, I'm gonna help you out ma. I'm gonna pay all of the tuition for your first year," he said.

Shock took over me. Deep down, I knew he was going to pay like half of it, but the whole year? Damn! I couldn't believe what I was hearing.

Yet just as he said that, his face became serious. "But there is one condition."

"What?" I asked.

"I'mma give you the money. Not because you my girl. I don't give free money to nobody. Not even my momma. This will be a loan. Either you pay me back plus interest within a year, or you do whatever I ask in exchange at all times. No excuses," he said coldly, throwing in the game changer.

Clearly I wasn't gonna be able to pay him back plus interest within a year, so I was gonna have to do whatever he say; but I didn't think it was going to be too bad.

I nodded my head and said, "Ok."

By the end of that night, Jerrod gave me the money in cash to put into my bank account when I left him. But that day, I learned that nothin' in this world was free. Even if he was your man, there are still terms and conditions attached.

~~~

The next couple of weeks flew by. My first year of tuition was paid for in full, and I was enjoying my summer of freedom. While I was out shopping at the mall with Danielle, my phone rang and of course it was Jerrod.

"Hey baby," I gleamed.

"Look, I got some shit that I need you and Dani to do," he said in a no nonsense tone.

"Oh, ok. What's that?" I asked as I watched Danielle come out the fitting room in a bomb ass red Herve Leger dress. I quickly gave her a thumbs up as Jerrod answered.

"I'm not about to disclose the details over the phone. You remember our agreement though. You do whatever I ask in exchange at all times. I know you and Dani are out at the mall, so wrap that shit up now and make your way to my house," he commanded. That was the first time he talked to me like that, and I didn't like it at all.

"Aiight fine. I'll see you then," I said before hanging up. Danielle noticed my sullen face expression as she walked out the dressing room in her regular clothes.

"What's wrong girl?" she asked.

"Remember what I told you about my agreement with Jerrod?" I began as we walked up to the register.

"Yeah, what about it?"

"He want me and you to come to his house and do something," I replied.

"Me? What he want me for?" she snapped as she laid her red dress on the counter.

"I don't know, but he said that I need to wrap this shopping shit up now and come to his house."

"Hmm, this must be some serious shit if he said that to you." Her eyebrow raised. "Well aiight, I'm down girl," she continued.

"Cool." I sighed. "Once you done paying for this we can head over there and find out what's going on."

"Aiight, bet," she simply stated before paying the blond woman at the register. Since she was dating KJ, the Reaper's right hand man, she was making money too. We were both living good and able to have whatever we wanted when we wanted. But, we would soon learn that with this lifestyle, came a hell of a price.

Danielle and I sat at the kitchen table across from Jerrod in silence as he began to explain what we were about to do.

"I need ya'll to go drop some shit off to my three locations. I got a black truck parked in the driveway with everything you need inside the trunk," he began, causing me to get nervous.

"You'll pull up to each location, get two duffel bags out for each, go up to the door and tell them Reaper sent you. They'll let you in and take it from there," he continued.

He stopped and looked at us for a second before he said, "Now it's too much product and money involved in all this, so don't fuck this up or that's yo' ass. Here's the addresses. Call me when you finish with the last drop." He slid the paper and car keys across the table.

"Ok," Danielle and I said in unison before getting up and heading out of the mansion.

I couldn't believe he was about to have us do something like this. But then again, I knew what he was into when I first started fuckin' with him. Now, here I was doing a drop for him that was risky as hell.

Danielle and I sat in silence as I carefully and cautiously drove to the location. If we got pulled over by the police that would be our asses, so I did my best to drive as safely as possible.

My heart rate increased as we pulled in front of the first trap house. "You ready?" I looked over to Danielle.

"As I'll ever be..." she sighed. "I just want to get this shit over with. I don't have a good feeling about this 'Tiva," she continued.

"I know.... It will be over soon enough. Let's do this shit," I replied before we hopped out of the car.

Making our way to the back of the SUV, I opened up the trunk only to see the six black duffel bags. As Danielle and I were grabbing the bags, I felt the cold barrel of a gun press against the back of my head.

"Don't fuckin' move bitch," the unfamiliar male voice said harshly. Fear took over me as me and Danielle stood there frozen.

"Grab them bags and turn around. No funny shit or yo' ass is dead!" he commanded.

Danielle and I turned around slowly only to see three guys standing there with guns in their hands and black masks covering their faces. With our hands trembling, we handed over the duffle bags, including the ones that were still in the trunk. After one of the men looked through the bags, making sure whatever that was in there was all there, he zipped the bags up and headed back to their car. The other two stood there with the guns still aimed at us. *This can't be happening right now!* Was all I could think as the third guy came back in front of us.

"What we going to do with them?" one of the guys said.

"Should we kill them?" the other guy said as his finger wrapped around the trigger, ready to shot.

The main guy that seemed to be the leader spoke again. "Naw. They don't seemed like they down with the Reaper like that. They probably some of his hoes."

"Yeah, they might be since they don't have any of his goons following them," the second man with the gun aimed at us chimed in.

"But it might be a set up!" the third guy urged.

"No it ain't no set up, I promise," Danielle pleaded.

"Shut yo' ass up!" the leader yelled as he placed his gun to Danielle's head.

"Please don't kill us, we only was doing what we was told! I promise if you take whatever is in that duffle bag we will leave here and not say anything," I begged.

"I don't think we can believe them. What if they lying just to run off to snitch to the Reaper," the second guy said, while eyeing us suspiciously.

The leader of the group look at us for a moment like he was thinking what their next move should be. After a couple of seconds he spoke again.

"Fuck it, let's go. We already know their faces, so if they were to snitch we can come back and kill their bitch asses."

He put his gun up, causing the other two men to follow suit. They followed him back to their vehicle and peeled off, just as quickly as they came.

Danielle and I were still in pure shock and fear after what happened. There was no way in hell we were going back to the Reaper's spot and telling him what happened. All I wanted to do was get the fuck home. Since there was a bus stop around the corner, we quickly made our way there and just our luck, a bus pulled up. We hopped on it and took it straight home. I bit my lip and sat there in silence, holding back the tears. I couldn't believe we got caught up in some shit like this. The shit that B-Moore told me that day at my locker replayed in my head. He was right, I'm not about that drug life, and I never wanted to be affiliated with that shit again. Once we got to my house, Danielle and I went straight up to my room, traumatized by what the fuck happened to us.

"What the fuck are we gonna do?" Danielle asked.

"I don't know…I mean, I can tell him we got robbed, so he can at least know what happened. But I can't deal with this shit anymore Dani," I cried.

"I can't be about that life with him. This is too much." I broke down.

"I know girl, I know." She hugged me. "Whatever you want to do, I'm with you," she reassured.

"Ok." I calmed down and grabbed my phone.

"We got robbed…I can't deal with this shit anymore. I'll give you your money when I have it. We're done" was all I texted Jerrod before blocking his number. As of now, Danielle and I would have to be low-key for a while.

~ ~ ~

A month passed, and Danielle and I stayed cooped up in the house until the coast was clear. From what we heard, the Reaper and his crew were in an all-out war with some new niggas that came here trying to take over. So I guess he found out who robbed him. Plus, if he really wanted to kill me or fuck me up for what happened, he would have done so already since he knew where Danielle and I lived. But it couldn't have been that deep, because we were the ones who got robbed. If anything, those who needed to face consequences were the ones who robbed us that night.

Finally out the house, Danielle and I decided to go to a party out in Columbus. Even though we decided to get out of the house, we still wanted to hang out as far away from Akron as possible. The cool night air felt so good as we hopped out of the car and began to make our way through the packed parking lot.

Out of nowhere two big, black men dressed in all black hopped out of an Escalade and made their way towards us. Before I could even react, one of the men snatched up Danielle and placed a black sack over her head. I turned, trying to run away, but the other man instantly tackled me to the ground and restrained me. I tried my best to get out his grasp, but he placed his knee into my back and tied my wrists with a zip tie.

"Let me the fuck go!" I screamed as I wiggled underneath the man, but he elbowed me in the back of my head, causing my head to spin. Placing a black sack over my head, he picked me up off the ground, placed me over his shoulders, and dumped me in the truck like I was a sack of trash.

As the car drove off, Danielle and I tumbled all over the back seat before the car stopped. I could hear Danielle starting to panic and whimper while I tried my best to remain calm. *What the fuck is going on?* was all I could think when the men snatched us out of the car.

After walking a little ways, the men shoved me into a seat and snatched the black sack off my head. I looked around as my vision came back, and from what I could tell, we were in some type of old abandoned warehouse by the look of the cobwebs and dust. I looked to my left to see Danielle, who was balling her eyes out. But no words came to mind to comfort her.

All I could hear was slow footsteps coming towards the area that Danielle and I were sitting in when the one man I thought I would never see came into view. There standing in front of us, was the man I used to know as Jerrod, but by his demeanor

I knew that we were dealing with the person the streets called the Reaper, dressed in all black with the hood of his hoodie up. Fear took over my body as I felt like I was looking death right in the face.

With his hands clasped in front of him, he looked like a judge that was about to serve us with a life sentence.

"So you thought you could just up and disappear after all that shit popped off? You really thought sending a fucking text was ok? You fucked up the one thing I had for you to do!" he began.

"Please Jerrod, let me explain," I started to say, but was met with a backhand slap to the face.

"Shut yo' bitch ass up! There is no need to explain any fucking thing!" he yelled. Hot tears fell from my eyes as he looked at me with pure anger and hate. I thought I would never see this side of him, but here I was, getting first-hand experience with why they called him the Reaper. I could feel the sharp pain of his slap still stinging on the side of my face as he cleared his throat before continuing.

"Now because of you two bitches fucking up the drop, I lost too much fucking money. And on top of that, we in a middle of a fucking war because of your little fuck up! Do you know how many of my niggas I had to fucking bury cause of you two?" He glared at us.

"So I sat back and thought about what type of compensation would possibly make up for all I've lost. And then it hit me...a body for a body," he explained a little too calmly. He motioned for one of the many men in the room to come to his side. The man handed the Reaper a pocket knife, which he flicked open and walked over to where Danielle and I sat.

"Now I'm feeling a little on the friendly side today since we had history. I know you couldn't offer up enough bodies for the ones I lost. So 'Tiva, it's your choice between you and Danielle. Which one of your bodies is going to compensate for my losses?" he said while lightly pressing the tip of the knife to Danielle's throat.

"Wait. Wait a minute Jerrod. There has to be another way we can fix this!" I said in a panic as Danielle cried.

"Naw 'Tiva, there is no other way. So I advise you to make a choice and make it quick, cause there is a lot of niggas in here who want to see ya'll both dead." He nodded to the group of niggas in the warehouse that seemed to keep multiplying.

"I can't...I can't do it. How am I supposed to choose which one of us dies?"

"Did any of my nigga's have a choice in who could live or die? Naw. Ya'll took their choice by fucking up the drop! Now fucking choose before I do!" he yelled.

Tears streamed down my face as I looked at Danielle, who started to plead for me not to choose her.

"No, no, no! You don't have to do this 'Tiva," she cried.

"Please Reaper...there got to be another way...please," she begged him.

"Shut the fuck up with all that cryin shit!" The Reaper gripped her hair tightly as he inched the knife closer to her neck, slightly breaking the skin and causing a little blood to come out.

Guilt and fear filled my body as I knew in my mind that the decision already had been made as soon as the Reaper put the deal on the table. I looked back at Danielle and mouthed sorry before telling him to take Danielle and not me.

A smirk of satisfaction came over his face as he threw Danielle to the floor and dragged her by her legs to a back room while whistling an unfamiliar tune. The men that once filled the room followed suit behind The Reaper. The moment they shut the door, the screams began. All you could here was the sounds of men brutally beating and raping Danielle as she begged for them to stop. This went on for what seemed like hours. Danielle's voice started to sound hoarse from all the screaming, but the next sound sent chills through my spine. A loud gunshot came from behind the door and everything went silent.

Reappearing from the room, the Reaper wiped his hands clean with a towel before coming my way. Without saying a word, he picked me up, placed me over his shoulder, and carried me out the building. Once out of the building, he placed me into the car next to him as the driver pulled off.

Within seconds we pulled up to Jerrod's mansion. Snatching me out the car and damn near dragging me into the house, Jerrod made his way to the bedroom. Tossing me onto the bed, and breaking off the zip tie that bound my hands together, he flipped me over on my back and grabbed my face violently.

"Take off your fucking clothes!" he barked as he let go of my face.

Without saying a word, I did what I was told. Once I was done undressing, Jerrod didn't waste no time stripping off his clothes and sliding in between my legs. He thrusted himself inside me and bucked wildly. Tears formed in my eyes as he ravished me, but my mind was elsewhere. I still couldn't believe that I was in this situation right now, and the fact that Jerrod made me play the act of God, and decide if my life was more important than Danielle's, was beyond sickening.

And that wasn't even the worst part. I was a complete monster to value my life more than Danielle's, when it was me who involved her in this mess. If only I hadn't ask Jerrod for that money, Danielle would still be alive. Jerrod finally finished and pulled out, cumming all over my face and body. He laid down next to me on the bed and rolled over before commanding me to go clean myself up and get back in the bed. I nodded in agreement, not wanting to anger him even further than I already had.

After getting out of the shower and putting on some clothes that I had left over at Jerrod's house, I made my way back into the bedroom only to see that he was fast asleep. *How the fuck could this nigga sleep so peacefully after all the bullshit he had done to me? How could this nigga sleep after having my best friend raped and killed?* I thought as I realized that he hadn't even noticed that I was back in the room.

He stirred slightly in his sleep, which caused me to hold my breath, hoping he didn't notice I wasn't in the bed. Realizing that he wasn't about to wake up, I knew I had to run while I had the chance. There was no telling what he had in mind to do with me once he was awake. I made my way down the steps and saw that Jerrod and I were the only ones in the mansion.

I sighed in relief since that made it easier for me to escape. All I knew was that I had to get the fuck out of here. But when I got to the front door, I stopped dead in my tracks. Where the fuck was I going to go? Even if I left here and went home, Jerrod could find me and drag me back here easily, and nobody would even care.

I got to get the fuck out of town! was the first thing that came to mind. But first I needed the money to be able to leave. I looked around and slowly crept my way into Jerrod's office, where his safe was at. After turning the dials, using the combination that I'd seen him continuously use before, I opened the safe and started to fill the duffle bag that was inside the safe with 50 grand that he had stashed inside.

Throwing the duffle bag over my shoulder, I walked back to the front door and slid out. Once outside I ran. I ran so fast that my lungs started to burn. By the time I made it to town, finally at the bus station, my legs felt like Jell-O. Out of breath, I made my way up to the ticket booth and purchased a bus ticket to ATL.

Once the bus pulled up, I grabbed the duffle bag of money and boarded the bus. Finding a seat in the back, I settled down with the duffle bag on my lap. I looked out the window as the bus pulled away. My thoughts wandered off, thinking about what ATL had in store for me. Shit, to be honest, I didn't care as long as I was far away from the Reaper. That day, I promised that I would never come back to Akron no matter what happened.

Present

I didn't know what had happened to the Reaper ever since then. No one out here even mentions his name. It was like he fell off the face of the earth. I didn't know if that was actually him in the crowd or my eyes playing tricks on me. Could be the guilt of the past finally haunting me. But all I know is, I'm going to continue being low-key for a while...just in case.

Chapter Three

Na'Tya

"Damn" was all I could say as I rolled over and caught my breath from the hot and steamy session me and Travis just had. It seemed like every time we connected, it just got better and better.

"Mmm." He pulled me into his arms. "I missed that good pussy," he whispered into my ear, causing me to giggle.

"This pussy missed you too baby."

"It better. Cause you know it's all mine," he said before kissing me on my neck. Lying here with Travis felt like pure bliss. We were spending this whole weekend together at the Ritz Carlton in Columbus, and after a hard and long week of working at the club, time with this sexy man was nothing but a treat.

"I could have this every day," he said, holding me tightly.

"Me too."

"I can't wait til' we make that happen baby. Every day, just you and me fuckin' all night and making breakfast for each other in the morning," he continued, causing a smile to form on my face at the thought.

"I could definitely work with that." I rolled over and planted a kiss onto his lips.

"Good," he said before getting on top of me and moving down between my legs. Yet right before he could give me some head, his phone began to ring.

"Hold on baby," he said as he hopped up and grabbed his phone. His smile quickly faded when he looked at the screen, and I knew exactly who it was.

"One moment..." he said to me before answering his phone and walking to the living room area of the suite. The moment of bliss was quickly put to an end when his wife called him.

By the time Travis came back, I was fully irritated. I sat up in the bed with my arms folded as he approached me.

"Let me guess, you gotta go huh?" I asked full of attitude.

"No, not yet." He sat next to me and kissed me on the cheek. "She said that she will be home tonight. So I will have to leave earlier than I thought," he confessed.

"Hmm, just like I thought," I coined in.

"Don't be like that 'Tya. Only a few more months and I'll be filing for divorce. Then after that's over with, it will be me and you. We'll finally be able to do the things we always wanted to do. No restrictions. We can do things like this every day in our new house." He said, selling me his pipe dream of him leaving his pretty little wife and finally being all mine.

Part of me wanted to believe it, but part of me knew it was bullshit. Yes I loved Travis, but I wasn't stupid. Men of his caliber didn't leave their wives that easily. He'd been with her for as long as he knew me, and from what I knew, they didn't have a prenup. So if he divorced her, she would be taking him to the fuckin' cleaners. With all the good things that were happening in my life, the last thing I needed was unnecessary drama over a nigga. If he stay with her...cool, if he doesn't...cool. Either way,

I'll be collecting my checks. I'll be good making my money from the strip club and from our escorting business. There are plenty of niggas that are out here checking for me, so when I'm ready to settle down, I'll decide who will get to be the lucky one to wife me up. As for now, I'mma just enjoy the ride.

The sound of a phone ringing broke my thoughts. This time it was my phone.

"Hold on Trav," I said before answering.

"Wassup 'Tiva?" I asked.

"Everything. I know that I said I was gonna be able to hold it down at the club tonight, but it's hectic over here. Seems like all hell is breaking loose," Na'Tiva explained.

"What? What's going on?" I asked in confusion.

"All these shipments are coming in. I don't know if you even authorized them or not. Me and the event planner is bumping heads, so you are going to have to deal with that bitch. The party promoter is havin' issues with the celebrity that's supposed to come tonight...it's too much," she sighed.

"Aiight. I'll be on my way" was all I could say before we hung up.

Tonight was a huge birthday bash for a celebrity hosted at my club, so tonight, everything had to go right. I looked over to my right only to see Travis examining me with his hazel eyes.

"So it seems like they need their boss lady to come and set things straight," he chuckled.

"Yeah, and I guess yo' wife need her husband home before she comes home tonight," I snapped back.

"Don't be like that 'Tya." I could see the sadness in his eyes, but at this point I didn't even give a fuck.

I rolled my eyes in response. "Look, as nice as this was, I gotta go. So I'll leave my key on the nightstand, and you can check us out when you get ready to leave to go see your prissy little bitch."

Travis couldn't even say one word. Instead, he sat in silence as he watched me get out of the bed and head to the bathroom so I could take a shower and get ready. The tension was thick in the air by the time I came out the bathroom fully dressed, and began to pack up my overnight bag. As soon as I placed the key on the nightstand, Travis finally spoke.

"I'm sorry that our weekend got ruined 'Tya. I'll make it up to you...I promise." He stood in front of me and wrapped his arms around my waist as he stared deeply into my eyes.

One look at his handsome face and I couldn't even help myself. No matter how mad I got at him for changing or cancelling his plans for his bitch, he always found a way to pull me back in. It was like he had a hold over me and I was addicted to his sexy ass.

"You betta'," I said, causing us to both chuckle.

"Mmm, you look so sexy when you angry." He licked his lips. "I'm ready to take yo' ass right here on the floor," he continued with his sexy voice, causing me to wet my panties.

"Boy you betta' stop! You know I gotta' go Trav. We'll have another time for all that," I said as I tried to break away from him.

"Another time huh? That's what I like to hear." He smiled before placing a kiss on my lips.

"Whateva'." I couldn't help but smile. "I'll see you later," I said as I grabbed my bag and headed out the door.

"Aiight. I'll make sure of that," he said as he stood in the doorway and watched my hips switching as I walked down the hall.

By the time I arrived at the club, I only had an hour to kill before the party was scheduled to start. As soon as I walked in, my boss mode was activated, taking care of our drink and food shipments and setting the event planner and party promoter straight.

"Now I don't want to hear nothing else. This shit has to be right or nobody is gettin' paid in this bitch but me, 'Tiva, and the strippers. You understand?" I said to both the event planner and the party promoter.

"Yes." They nodded.

"This party is going to be great. No problems. I promise." Takia, the event planner, reassured.

"It better. Or that's your asses. Now I have my staff that I need to attend to," I replied, before walking away leaving them dumbfounded by my no-nonsense approach. Picking up the microphone off the bottom step, I stepped on the stage and began to talk to the rest of my team.

"Can everyone gather around the stage please? We have some important stuff to go over before the party starts," I announced. Everyone quickly gathered around the stage, giving me their full attention as I began to explain the basic rules for tonight.

"Now tonight is very important. I want you guys to put your best foot forward tonight. Martez, Glenn, and Gina, ya'll have to make sure the drinks are in full supply and keep them comin'. It's about to be a full house so we got to keep them happy," I explained, before I looked over to my team of professionally dressed cocktail waitresses, and then to my team of sexy bottle girls.

"Now you already know what is expected of you girls. We have a tight system on presenting the drinks and getting them to the customers on time. So if you stick with that, there shouldn't be no problems," I directed to them. All of them nodded in agreement, causing a smirk of satisfaction to cover my face.

"And now to my dancers..." I turned to my left and faced Honey, Diva, and the rest of my many strippers.

"I want ya'll to go harder than you ever did before. We got some major heavy hittas' that's gonna be here tonight, and we want them to make all they paper rain on this stage and at the booths you dancin' at," I began.

"Can't be no half steppin' tonight. No gettin' tired and running to the back taking long breaks. Tonight we have to be on it and make this the best party we ever had. I'm not accepting no B.S. and will not hesitate to cut you loose if you fuck up," I said shrewdly.

"What? Whatchu' mean you gonna cut us loose if we fuck up? Ain't nobody gonna cut me loose that's for sure, cause without me it wouldn't be no club," Honey snapped.

"Excuse me?" My eyebrow quickly raised.

"You heard me! I knew yo' ass when you didn't have shit and had to turn to strippin', thanks to me. Now you over here thinking you the fucking queen of Akron, just cause you opened up this fuckin' club off of Buck's money. Bitch who you foolin'!" Honey challenged.

Before I even realized it, I jumped up and grabbed that bitch by her throat.

"Bitch who the fuck do you think you talkin' to like that? This is my mothafuckin' establishment, and I'll be damned if I let a bitch come up in here and disrespect me in my fuckin' shit! You got me fucked up. I brought yo' ass up in this shit to work for me. And if you keep fuckin' up and disrespectin' me, I'll take yo' fuckin' hoe ass out!" I threatened as my grip tightened around her neck.

Na'Tiva

I couldn't believe my eyes as I stood there and watched 'Tya jump up and choke Honey. The rest of the staff were in just as much shock as me, as I could see the horror stretched across their faces. I knew that Honey was out of line for what she said, but I didn't think that my sister would snap like that. Without a second thought, I jumped up and pulled 'Tya off of our dancer.

"Naw, get off me!" 'Tya yelled as I pulled her to the other side of the stage. "That bitch got me fucked up!"

"Calm down 'Tya!" I yelled back. "It's too much money on the table tonight for this petty shit." I glanced at both Honey and 'Tya. "Honey, go into the dressing room and go clean yourself up. You need to calm down and get yourself together for tonight.

And if you try to pull some stuff like that again your ass is fired!" I commanded.

"Fine!" she said as the security guard released her to go to the dressing room. I looked over to our staff and demanded them to get to their stations and prepare for the party. I watched as they quickly scattered off before I turned and focused my attention back to a fuming 'Tya.

"Don't let her get you out of character. You own this club. You are the businesswoman, not her. You can't let some rat bitch come up in here and fuck up what you worked so hard for," I continued, snapping her back into reality.

'Tya stood there, slowly calming down as my words sunk in. She nodded her head, letting me know that she was feeling what I said to her.

"You're right. I let that bitch get me out of character," she finally said.

"Yeah. We can't let that happen though. Tonight is a big night. So let's go have a quick drink upstairs and let's get to this money," I suggested, causing her to smirk.

"Aiight girl. Let's get to this money," she agreed before we stepped off the stage and made our way to our office.

We enjoyed our last ten minutes before the party began over some strong martinis, made by our bartender. I had to keep my sister calm because if she wasn't in the right mood, the entire event could be at risk. Yet once the party began, it was as if nothing happened at our meeting with the staff. The night was a success!

That one party generated more income than we would produce in a month, and we were already planning for more.

"We did that bitch!" 'Tya danced in the doorway of our office.

"We sure did." I smiled.

"I can't even wait for the next one. We about to make so much fuckin' money! It's about to be crazy!" Na'Tya exclaimed.

"I know. It's about to be a goodass month," I replied as I got up and began to gather my things.

"You not staying for the staff after-party?" she asked.

"No girl. I'm tired...plus you know I don't do the whole after-party thing," I answered before we headed down the stairs.

"Oh aiight. Well call me or text me when you get home," 'Tya replied before we gave each other a hug and went our separate ways.

I stepped into the empty, dark parking structure and made my way to the car. I gripped my cellphone tighter in my hand as a sense of fear began to come over me. I don't know why, but I got a strange feeling that someone was following me. It was as if there was a strong presence looming in the darkness, even though there was no one else in the parking structure other than me. I sped up the pace of my stride as I began to get closer to my car, which was parked at the far end of the second level. Yet the eerie feeling grew stronger. Rapidly, I turned around in the middle of the structure, looking to see who was behind me, but there was no one there.

T.L. Joy

I let out a sigh as I got to my car and hopped in. *Maybe I'm just trippin' again. Maybe I'm just paranoid,* I thought to myself as I pulled out of the parking lot and made my exit. *Or maybe someone was really following me*? I didn't know what the fuck was going on, but I could feel myself slowly going crazy. I know that I'd been low-key ever since that one night in the club...that one night where I thought I saw that familiar face out in the crowd weeks ago. But maybe even working here at the club was making things worse for me.

Once I got home, I double checked the locks on the doors and windows. I sent 'Tya a quick text to let her know I was at the house before I locked myself in my room and said a prayer, praying that the Lord protects me from the evil that may lurk in the darkness.

103

Na'Tya

I was still on cloud nine after last night's success when I walked into my office, hours before the club opened to the public. I began to work on some paperwork for all of our upcoming events when loud knocks on the door interrupted my flow.

"Come in," I yelled out, but I wished I'd never said that when the door opened, revealing Honey's bitch ass.

"What do you want?" I asked sternly.

"I-I just wanted to talk, 'Tya," she said softly as she stepped into the office and closed the door behind her.

"You can keep the door open," I replied, with a raised eyebrow of suspicion.

"Oh, ok," Honey said dryly as she backtracked and opened the door. I watched her closely as she sat in the leather chair in front of my desk.

"So what is going on?" I asked.

"I wanted to talk about last night..." she paused and looked up at me with pleading eyes.

"What about it?" I said coldly.

"I know it got out of hand. But a bitch is feelin' some type of way. I mean, I brought you in this game to help you make money. And yeah, you been doin' numbers and shit. Even got on Buck's Fab Five. I can't be mad at you for doing what you got to do to make it to the top and shit, but you can't forget about ya' girl like that," she continued.

I sat back in my chair, folding my arms across my chest as I just looked at her for a minute. "Ok..."

Her face scrunched up from my one word response. "I'm just sayin', you ova' here owning a club and shit, making all this fuckin' money, and ain't even thought about letting me get in on it. Not even letting me have a role in the business other than being a fuckin' stripper," she snapped.

"Instead you gonna' just turn around and let yo' sister be your fuckin' business partner. The same fuckin' sister who left yo' ass high and dry back in high school. Who didn't give two fucks that you and ya' mama was out here strugglin'. What type of shit is that 'Tya? My ass been there for you no matter what! I helped you get on and make this money. I linked yo' ass up with connects and this is how the fuck you repay yo' best friend?" she continued, but it fell upon deaf ears.

I got so tired of bitches and niggas from my past wanting fuckin' handouts when they wasn't willing to get off their fuckin' lazy asses and try to do better for their damn selves. Instead they were stuck being content with they basic ass lives, but got the nerve to come to me and act like how dare I do something to better my fuckin' self! Wanting me to just give them shit that I sacrificed and worked too fuckin' hard for. At this point, they could all kiss my ass!

"Are you listening to what the fuck I'm sayin' to you bitch!" Honey yelled, snapping me out of my thoughts.

"Bitch? Here you go with that shit Honey," I began. "Don't come up in my office just to start shit and disrespect me. I told yo' ass last time that I brought you in to be on my team, and I'll take yo' ass out if you keep disrespectin' me."

"Fuck you bitch! I'll come all up and through shit and fuck yo' ass up." Honey jumped up out of her seat. "No matter how many fuckin' businesses you own, you ain't nothing but a hoodrat bitch that fucked 'n' sucked her way to the top. Yo' momma would roll over in the grave if she knew all the fucked up shit you done," she sneered, causing my blood to boil. Before I could say anything else, she hacked up a thick glob of spit that landed on my desk.

"Fuck you and yo' establishment. I'm out this bitch!" she yelled, and in one swift motion, she turned around and walked out of my office. Before I could get out of my seat and get to her, she was already at the bottom step.

I thought about what 'Tiva said about not letting this bitch get me out of my character, but Honey had fucked up one last time. She might've gotten away with this one, but I got something for her ass.

~~~

Later that night, I knew exactly where Honey would be if she wasn't at my spot. Word around town was that she was fuckin' around with one of my old clients for money. She told all her little friends at the beauty shop about her rich, white sugar daddy. Bitch couldn't even hustle right. She always had to run her mouth, making it easy for me and my crew of niggas to slide right in as she was walking out the hotel. As soon as she got close to her car in the parking lot, my righthand man, Deuce, grabbed her and pulled her ass in our black van.

"What the fuck!" she screamed as we took off, but was quickly silenced when she seen my gun pointed at her head.

"Got something else to say now bitch?" I said with a smirk planted on my face. She sat there in shock as she shook her head 'no'.

"That's what the fuck I thought," I said as our car parked.

"Get this bitch out of here!" I commanded as my men grabbed Honey and dragged her ass out the van and pulled her into the dark alley.

I stood in front of her as my two men made her drop down onto her knees.

"Please 'Tya! It ain't that deep to have to do this," she cried. "I-I-didn't mean to-" she began, but was abruptly cut off when I smacked the shit out her with the butt of my gun.

"Shut the fuck up bitch! You done said enough shit up in my office today and I don't wanna' hear shit else you got to say," I yelled angrily.

"Did you really think I was gonna let yo' hoe ass get away with sayin' that shit to me? You got some fuckin' nerves bitch, to be up in my place of business and disrespect me? You lost yo' fuckin' mind!" I snapped before smackin' her across the face once again, causing blood to fly out of her mouth.

"Pleaseeee! Please don't kill me...I'm sorry," she pleaded, bloody mouth and all.

I laughed wildly at her pleas. "Bitch! Yo' ass wasn't thinkin' about apologizing when you was talkin' all that shit."

"No, I was just mad...I'm sorry...Please don't do this ... Please 'Tya don't do-" she began, but was silenced when I pulled the trigger and shot her in the head. As she laid on the ground, I released a full clip into her body.

"You stupid fuckin' bitch! You won't be talkin' that shit now," I yelled out as I stood over her lifeless body. I examined what I had done as I grimmed the fuck out of her for one last time. Tossing the gun over to Deuce, I took off my black surgical gloves that we all had on.

"Take care of this shit and get rid of the evidence," I commanded before I cautiously walked out of the alley and headed to my car that was a block away.

A smile of satisfaction spread over my face as I drove home. Now that Honey's ass was gone, there would be no more problems.

Chapter Four

Na'Tya

I woke up in the plush bed wrapped in Travis's arms. I couldn't help but smile as I enjoyed this tranquil silence in our suite. His wife was out of town for two weeks due to work, and 'Tiva had hired us a manager to make sure our business would be taken care of while we both took some time off. Everything had been so peaceful since my one little problem was taken care of, and I wouldn't have it any other way.

"Good morning," Travis greeted before kissing me on my shoulder. "You have a good sleep?" he asked.

"You already know." I turned towards him and kissed him on his lips.

"Good. I'm about to hop in the shower. Join me when you're ready." Travis winked before getting up and heading to the bathroom. I laid there admired his sexy naked body as he walked away. Yet, all of my dirty thoughts were abruptly interrupted by my phone vibrating on the nightstand.

"What the hell?" I said out loud as I grabbed my phone and opened up one of the many incoming text messages.

LOOK AT THE LOCAL NEWS RIGHT NOW!

Read one of the text messages from Crystal, another one of my best dancers from the club. Curiosity took over me as I turned on the TV and went to our local news station. Immediately, my body turned cold as I seen a picture of Honey's face next to the caption, "POPULAR STRIPPER GONE MISSING!"

I sat up in the bed, stunned as the news reporter began to explain how Honey's family was pushing this search to find her. They wanted anybody who knew what happened the last day they seen her a week ago to speak up, while investigators were working closely on this case. My stomach churned as they showed the picture of my strip club as the last place Honey was reported to be seen before she went missing. Not only was this bringing bad press to my club, but I had a feeling that this shit was not going to turn out too well. At that moment, I knew that I had a whole new set of problems on my hands.

Na'Tiva

"Alright, now that everything is set, it should be smooth sailing for you," I said to our new manager as we sat in our office going over our automated computer system.

"Yes, we should be good." Monica flashed me a Colgate smile. "Thanks so much for the opportunity," she continued.

"No problem. If you need anything, just call my cell." I suggested as I grabbed my purse off my desk and walked over to the door.

"Sure will. Have a nice day Na'Tiva," Monica replied professionally.

"You too. Goodbye Monica," I said before making my exit. I was so glad that we hired a skilled and professional woman to manage our business to take off the workload. After all this crazy shit I been going through, I needed to have some time off and get my mind right, starting today!

Walking out of the club, I made my way towards my car. I looked around the almost empty parking structure as the feeling of being watched crept over me again. I stopped in my tracks and looked around again and saw nothing. "Calm down 'Tiva, you're just tripping," I said out loud to myself as I started to walk again to my car.

Once at the car, I took my keys out my purse to unlock the door. In the reflection of the car window, a shadowy figure appeared behind me. Before I could move, they placed a handkerchief over my mouth and nose.

The smell of chloroform filled my mouth and nostrils. With my best effort, I tried to fight off the person, but their grip only tightened. My head started to spin and my body started to feel weak. As my knees buckled beneath me, everything faded to black.

When I regained consciousness, I was tied up in the back seat of a car. With my vision still slightly blurry, I could make out two people in the front seat. But what I heard next shook me to the core. A familiar tune being whistled from the front seat sent chills all throughout my body. *It couldn't be him! No Lord, please let it not be him!* I screamed loudly inside my head.

My vision was now clear when I saw the face of the man that I wished I would never see again. There in the passenger seat of the car was the Reaper! He sat there whistling that tune over and over again as tears formed in my eyes. *He's going to kill me! Oh God, He's going to fucking kill me!* I repeated over and over again in my thoughts. My silent tears turned into loud whimpers, causing the Reaper to turn around.

"Shut yo' ass up bitch!" he commanded as he pulled out his gun. " I ain't playing games with yo' ass either. Make another fucking sound and I'mma' blow yo fuckin' head off!" he snapped.

I lightly bit my lip and started to sniffle in my best efforts to hold in my cries. Never in a million years did I think the Reaper would come after me. I looked out the window as we rode down the street and came up to an old, rundown mental institution. Pulling around the back, the Reaper and his driver got out of the car. The driver flung open my door and snatched me out the car and forced me to follow behind the Reaper.

Once inside the worn down building, we passed room after room until we reached the main office. The driver shoved me into a chair and started to strap me into shackles so I couldn't move. Once he was finished, he left the room, leaving me alone with the Reaper.

The Reaper stood in front of the desk with a devilish grin before he started to speak. "Bet you thought you would never see me again huh?" he chuckled.

"What do you want Jer..." I started to speak only to be hit with the butt of the Reaper's gun, so hard my face started to throb.

"I ain't tell yo fuckin ass to speak! You shut the fuck up while I'm speaking! You think I want to hear anything yo ass have to say after you stole from me and ran? And you know what the funny thing is? The fact your stupid ass thought you got away with the shit!" he began.

"I knew the whole fucking time yo' ass ran off with my money to Atlanta. Down there living the good life off my mothafuckin' money. I thought you woulda knew better than that 'Tiva, especially after what happened to your little friend Danielle. So I figured to let you have a little fun, but you started to get a little too cocky for your own good. So I had to humble yo' ass real quick. Man, I feel a little bit bad killin' yo' mom like that, but shit, bitch had to go," he said simply.

"You bitch mothafucka'! You killed my momma you sick twisted son of a bitch!" I screamed in rage. "She ain't have shit to do with nothing! You ain't have to kill her like that!"

The Reaper looked at me with a cold blank stare before grabbing my face. He gripped my face so hard that my jaw started to hurt.

"Didn't I tell yo ass to shut the hell up! Yo mom died because of you, just like Danielle! You a stupid bitch thinking you can run with someone else's money and not pay the cost. Bitch you forgot who the fuck I was!" he yelled before shifting his hand down to my throat and started to choke me.

" I shoulda killed yo' ass a long time ago, but a nigga had feelings for yo' ass. So I tried to let you slide...just for you to turn around and stab me in the back again. But not this time Tiva. See, this time a nigga ain't going to let feelings get in the way of business. I'mma enjoy killing you nice and slow," he stated, before slowly loosening his grip from around my neck.

The Reaper stepped back towards the desk before yelling for his driver to come back in.

"Take her to the killing room. I got something to handle before dealing with her," he ordered before walking out of the room. Unshackling me from the chair, the driver snatched me up and dragged me out the room and back down the hall to the stairwell.

Pushing me forward, he made me descend down the dark stairway toward the basement of the building. Once at the bottom of the steps, there down the dimly lit hallway was a room. Nudging me forward, we made our way to the door. The driver opened the door, and what I saw inside the killing room made me think of all the horror movies I'd seen when I was a child.

Inside the room there was a man, hoisted up by his arms from the ceiling, in shackles. The man was all bloody and bruised up and didn't even attempt to move. The driver knocked me to the ground before leaving the room, and shutting the door.

I scooted up against the wall to balance myself as I sat up. With my hands still tied behind my back, I looked up at the man before calling out to him.

"Aye...aye nigga, you dead?" I whispered. The man groaned, letting me know he wasn't dead. I sighed in relief as he slowly looked my way, and to my surprise, there above me was an old acquaintance of mine from when I was dating B-Moore back in the day.

"Gunz, that you?" I asked, a little puzzled at the fact that he was here in the killing room.

"Tiva? What the fuck you doing here?" he barely choked out.

"Shit, I was just about to ask you that. How long you been down here?"

"Shit, a couple months maybe…"

"A couple months! What the fuck you do that made the Reaper come after you?"

"Shit, don't even worry about all that. You need to worry about gettin' the fuck outta here before the Reaper come back," he urged.

Sitting there, I knew he was right. If I was still in this room when the Reaper got back, I was as good as dead. I refused to end up dead just like the rest of his victims. Right then and there, my survival mode kicked in. Surveying the room, I saw a vent in the far corner, so I started to slide across the wall and made my way toward it. I'd only seen this in movies, but shit, a bitch was strapped for time, so giving this a try wouldn't hurt anything. Scooting in front of the vent, I started to kick at it. After a couple of minutes I busted a hole in the vent, leaving a couple of jagged edges.

Turning around, I placed my hands around the jagged edge and started to rub the zip tie against it, in an attempt to cut myself loose. Just as the zip tie loosened, I heard footsteps coming towards the door. I moved my hands up and down quickly, cutting myself loose before the door swung open. The Reaper walked into the room with a crazed look on his face.

"I see you made yourself comfortable," he said as he walked towards me. With my hands still behind my back, I grabbed ahold of one of the jagged edges and started to twist it, trying to pry it loose. The jagged edge cut into my hands as I gripped it tightly until I could feel it bend.

"Don't worry 'Tiva, I'll make sure I take my time with you," he chuckled as he was inches away from me. I mustered as much strength as I had and finally snapped a piece of the vent off and held it in my hand. The Reaper lunged at me, aiming for my neck, but I pulled out the piece of the vent and jabbed it into his eye.

The Reaper fell screaming in pain as I hopped off the ground and made my way over to the switch that controlled the shackles. Flipping the switch on, I lowered Gunz to the ground and unhooked him. The Reaper rolled on the ground, screaming in agony as I propped Gunz up against my shoulder and walked out the room. Walking down the dimly lit hallway, I saw an emergency exit.

We was almost to the exit when the sound of people running down the staircase filled my ears. *We have to hurry and get the fuck outta' here!* I thought as my pace quickened.

Finally making it to the emergency exit, I fell into the door as I pushed it open while dragging Gunz along. Walking up to the first car I saw, gunshots started to ring out behind us. Ducking and dodging the best I could, I opened the car door and dropped Gunz into the passenger seat. Running to the other side of the car, I hopped in and started to kick at the bottom of the steering wheel to expose the wires so I could hot-wire the car.

Bullets flew into the car as I ducked down and started to fiddle with the wires. Gunz cried out in pain as one of the bullets hit him in the leg. "Hurry the fuck up 'Tiva!" he urged as I finally got the car to start. Sitting back up, I pulled the gear shift into drive and slammed on the gas, sending the car flying forward. Peeling out of the mental institution parking lot, I sped down the street.

Doing over 100 miles per hour, I drove down the street like a mad women. I finally slowed down after making sure I was far enough away from the building.

"We got to ditch the car. You know somewhere we can go?" I asked Gunz as I hit another corner.

"Yeah. Stop the car over there and we can walk to this stash spot I know," Gunz said while pointing to a vacant parking lot.

After ditching the car, I helped Gunz out and walked a couple blocks down to the stash spot. A young nigga ran out the building and started to talk to Gunz.

"What the fuck happened?" the guy said.

"Got into some shit. We need a whip to get the fuck outta here Cash!" Gunz said in pain.

"Aiight hold on," Cash said before he ran to the back of the house and came back to the front in a car. We hopped into the car before Cash hurriedly drove off.

I sat in the back seat, looking out the back window to make sure we weren't being followed.

After we were miles away from Akron, I finally sat back and took a deep breath. I wasn't sure where we were going, but all I knew was that I was glad we got out of that hell hole alive. We jumped on the interstate, and an hour and a couple of minutes later, we passed a sign that said "Welcome to Pittsburgh, Pennsylvania."

I looked around as we exited off the interstate and onto a service drive. Within a couple of minutes, we were pulling up to a tall iron gate. Cash punched in a code and the gate slowly opened up. Driving up a long driveway you saw nothing but trees. With all the trees, you would have thought we were in the middle of the woods.

Finally reaching our destination, there stood a big mansion filled with armed guards with AK-47s. When we pulled into the circular driveway in front of the mansion, there stood a woman in a pant suit outfit like she had known that we were on our way.

After exiting the car, we walked up to the mansion and entered. The woman guided me to the living room while Cash and Gunz walked straight up the steps. I sat down on the leather loveseat and looked around the room, noticing how nicely the house was decorated.

The woman who guided me into the living room informed me that this was where I would be staying for the night. After handing me a blanket and a pillow, she left me there in the living room alone. A little bothered by how I was brought into a mansion and left alone to sleep on a couch, made it difficult for me to sleep. But after a couple of minutes of reflecting on all that had happened tonight, I realized how lucky I was to just be alive to see another day. I curled up on the loveseat and fell into a deep sleep.

Chapter Five

Na'Tiva

The loud ringing of my cell phone woke me up. Surprised that it still had some charge left after last night, I rose up from the couch and grabbed it off the coffee table.

"Hello..." I answered groggily.

"Where the fuck you been? Everyone's been calling me about Honey missing and all this bad press we been gettin. I been texting yo' ass all night and haven't heard from you. You been blowing me off huh bitch?" 'Tya ranted.

"No, I wasn't blowing you off. I just...ran into a new friend and was spending time with him," I lied. There was no way I was about to tell her about the

Reaper, especially with all this other shit that was going on at the club.

"Ohhh! Yo' ass was getting yo' groove on last night huh?" she joked. "I see you girl. I ain't mad at you. We all need a nice supply of vitamin D every now and then. Well I just wanted to make sure you alive and well since I haven't heard from you. But now that I know, I'll let you carry on," 'Tya continued.

"Ok. I'll talk to you later," I replied before we hung up.

As soon as I sat my phone back down on the table, Gunz entered the living room. Compared to how he looked last night when I first seen him in the Reaper's killing room, he looked as if he healed overnight.

His smooth brown skin was no longer bloody, but the scars and minor bruises still remained. His thick black hair was now cut in low waves and his facial hair was trimmed. I figured they took care of his bullet wound since he was now hopping around on his own. He was now looking like the Gunz I remembered from back in the day.

"You hungry?" was all he asked.

"Yeah."

"Aiight, come with me. One of the cooks made breakfast," he replied before leading me down the large hallway to the kitchen.

"So is this all you?" I asked as I looked at the expensive art on the wall.

"Naw, this is one of the houses for our affiliation. Something like a safe house," he said nonchalantly as we walked into the kitchen.

"Oh ok," I replied, taking a seat at the kitchen island. Gunz grabbed the two plates full of breakfast food off the kitchen counter before taking a seat next to me.

We ate in silence for a minute before he finally spoke.

"Thank you...you could've been like some bitch niggas and just left me there, but you looked out for a nigga and now we lived to see another day."

"Shit, thank you for linking up with your connections to get out of Akron," I redirected.

"Who would've thought I'd see yo' ass under these circumstances...right when we was both facin' death. Last time I seen yo' ass, you was still with that nigga Brandon," he said, bringing up the blast from the past.

"Speaking of Brandon, what happened with you and that nigga?" I asked curiously, hoping that he could give me some info on Brandon that would lead me straight to him and get my revenge.

Gunz shook his head as a look of disgust covered his face. "It's because of that nigga that I got caught up with the Reaper in the first fuckin' place."

"What?" I almost choked on my orange juice.

"Back when Reaper was in his prime, me and B was on the come up. Niggas got tired of being broke, but we didn't want to be up under the Reaper. At that time, this little Haitian broad I was fuckin' with told me that her brother had connections, and if we wanted work she'd hook me and B up. We hopped on that shit, but first, we had to get rid of the competition. So we did some shit to push Reaper's ass out and took ova'. Since then we been movin' heavy weight and making bank," Gunz explained.

I wanted to ask more questions, but before I could say anything else, Gunz continued.

"Brandon wanted to have a legal business on top of the drug money, so he took ova' his pop's shit and made more money off that. It was all good ya' know? We had the streets on lock and the business shit on lock too. But then B got greedy and started fuckin' everyone over. He got his own connect and started to compete, cutting me and our main connect completely out. He started taking clients from other affiliations that had their own designated city. I know what we did to Reaper was fucked up, but that was a part of the game. After that we made sure we played by the rules. But Brandon was still on that otha' shit. The nigga started a war out there on these streets, and since we came into this shit together, they started to come for me too. Business got all fucked up, and then this nigga got the nerve to fake his own fuckin' death?"

"I know...I was in the car with him when it happened," I chimed in.

"You was there?" His eyebrow raised in suspicion.

I didn't want him to think I was tied to Brandon and lose his trust in me, so I told him everything. From the time I touched down in Ohio to now.

"Damn ma'," was all Gunz could say. I looked down in shame as I could feel his eyes closely observing my scars and keloids on my face.

"That's fucked up. I swear we gonna fuck up that nigga when we find his ass," he said.

"You know where he is?" I asked.

"Not yet, but my connect got his men searching for his ass. We been getting close, but he always switch up to another location by the time we get there. But that nigga for damn sure is alive and well. Believe dat!" Gunz snapped.

"That bitch nigga!" I sneered.

"Now with Brandon disappearing when he did, business went under and he left his connects high and dry, owing them money and leaving his clientele feining. Then with my ass being locked up at the Reapers spot for so long, we all fucked up in the game. We need a new route to move our products to the clients, but that ain't so hot cause the streets is a fuckin' war zone," Gunz confided in me.

"If I don't get this shit settled, then the connect is gonna come for my ass thinkin' I'm in on Brandon's fucked up plan...fuck!" He slammed his fist down onto the white marble countertop.

I sat there in silence as I watched as he placed his face in his palms out of frustration.

At that moment, I knew this was a perfect opportunity for me to link up with Gunz and his connect.

"I might have a way.... Me and 'Tya opened up this strip club that is getting hella' traffic and is making tons of money," I began, causing Gunz to lift his head and listen attentively.

"We could move the work in my club. Maybe create an underground route. And I could provide a possible group of large clientele, on top of your own, to use the product. I'll even pay the connect back what Brandon owes plus more," I suggested.

Gunz sat back in his seat and rubbed his chin. "Hmm. And what you want out the deal?" he asked.

"The only thing I want in return is their loyalty, and to be brought in on this search for Brandon. I want to be the one to put the bullet in that nigga's head," I replied.

Gunz smiled. "Aiight, that sounds good. Now what about the percentage for movin' weight up in your club?" he asked, getting straight to the point.

"I'll talk about that with your connect," I shot back.

"Nah...I'll talk to him on your behalf. The connect is very serious on who comes close to him, so I'll have to see if the connect is with it and we go from there," Gunz explained.

"Ok. That's fine," I agreed.

"Good. We're gonna' stay here for a couple of days until the coast is clear with the Reaper. Let me show you to your room upstairs," Gunz said while getting out of his seat.

"Oh, so I get a room now huh?" I said sarcastically.

"Sorry about 'dat. It's all a part of protocol. Gotta make sure you trustworthy first. Now c'mon. I know yo' ass need a shower," he joked.

"Whateva'!" I said as I got up and followed him upstairs to my room.

As I hopped in the shower under the warm running water, all I could think about was the deal I struck up with Gunz.

If I could get the connect to agree to this deal and give me a good percentage out of the sales, then I knew I could rack up more money and have a team behind me to help find and kill B-Moore.

Na'Tya

"We have some investigators here wanting to ask the staff and you some questions about Honey," our manager, Monica, said frantically over the phone.

"Alright. I'm on my way," I said, before ending our conversation.

I rolled my eyes in irritation before hopping out of bed and getting dressed. So much for a relaxing getaway with Travis.

"Problems at the club?" he asked as he walked out of the bathroom in nothing but a towel.

"Yes. All because of Honey's ass," I sighed in frustration.

"You should've called me and I would have handled it. I don't know why you tried to take matters into your own hands with this one..." he began to lecture me.

"Look, I got this. They haven't found her body yet, so my team did a damn good job," I cut him off.

"Oh really? Then why are investigators at your club wanting you to come in for questioning?" he darted back.

"I mean she did work for me, and we did get into it at the club...in front of everyone," I said slowly, feeling the regret of all that had happened before she died.

"Not a good look 'Tya...but we went over the questioning protocol. So you should be good. If not..." he paused and looked at me with a stern face. "If not, I'll have to do my best to clean this shit up," Travis continued.

"Good, but I won't fuck up." I smiled and kissed him on the cheek.

"See you when I get back," I continued before I grabbed my designer bag and car keys off the dresser and made my exit.

It was time to handle this shit once and for all.

~ ~ ~

As soon as I walked into the club, I was immediately greeted by a panicked Monica, followed by two men dressed in black suits. *Here it comes,* I thought to myself.

"Na'Tya, this is Detective Connors and Detective Logan, and this is our owner Na'Tya," she introduced nervously.

"We got it from here. Thank you Ms. Johnson," the tall gray haired man said firmly.

"No problem," she replied before walking away, leaving me with the two men.

"How may I help you two?" I asked, switching on my professional demeanor.

"We are here to see if you can come in for questioning. We talked to most of your staff and wanted to go over some of the details with you."

Part of me wanted to say hell no, but I knew that the sooner I took care of this shit, the better. Especially for the sake of my business. All this bad press was slowly killing our reputation.

"Ok. I have a few things that I need to do here for our event. Can I come in shortly after that?" I asked.

"Sure. Here is our card and information. We'll see you then," Detective Connors, the tall, older man said.

"Ok. See you then." I smiled and held opened the door for them as they walked out. I watched as they pulled out of the parking lot before I headed upstairs and went over what I was going to say to them during their interrogation. I needed some extra time to prepare, and plus, I didn't want to be seen in the back of their cop car. Even if it was just to come in for questioning, people loved to gossip, and the last thing I needed was speculation on my involvement in Honey's case.

Once I felt confident in my answers to possible questions, I left the club and headed to the police office.

I tried to remain as calm as possible as I sat across from the two men. They began asking me basic questions, such as how long have I known Honey and when did she start working for me. They kept it pretty light until they asked me the real questions.

"So, many of your staff members reported that you and Ms. Briggs had a scuffle at the club the night before her disappearance. Is that correct?" Detective Connors asked.

"Yes," I simply stated.

"What caused it?" Detective Logan chimed in.

"I was having a meeting with the staff before our event, and she rudely interrupted me and said some disrespectful and derogatory things, which is really unlike her," I answered, playing my role of a concerned employer and friend.

"I see," Detective Logan replied.

"But this wasn't just any regular spat. You got physical with her, right Ms. Davis?" Detective Connors pushed.

"Unfortunately I slipped out of character, yes...but it wasn't a full-on fight," I said, but immediately regretted saying it.

Damnit! I could feel myself losing my control over this interrogation. *Pull it together 'Tya!*

"You slipped out of character..." Detective Connors repeated. "So did you guys talk about what happened the next day?" he asked.

"She did come to my office to apologize for her actions at our meeting," I answered.

"And about what time was that?" Detective Logan asked, while holding a small yellow notepad and pen in his hand.

"Umm, about three o' clock. She came hours before our club opened to the public."

"Did you guys have another argument while she was in your office?" Detective Connors asked. I was starting to hate this man and his fucking questions, but I rubbed my hands together to keep myself calm and spoke.

"No. She explained that she'd been stressed and having relationship issues with her boyfriend, and she apologized for her actions. She also asked to take some time off," I lied through my teeth.

"Oh really?" Detective Connors's eyebrow raised.

"Do you know who she was in a relationship with?" Detective Logan asked.

"I don't know his name, but from what she briefly said from time to time, he was an older Caucasian man who was an executive at an investment firm. I know that she was happy that he would help provide for her household, but that's all

I know." I lightly shook my head and looked at them innocently. Deep inside, I was jumping for joy that I was able to direct their attention to another possible suspect.

"Ok. We have to step out for a minute Ms. Davis, but we will be back. We still have a few more questions. Can you give us a minute please?" Detective Connors said.

"Ok," was all I said before the two men left the room. Just when I thought this shit was over, they still had more fucking questions. I could feel my patience running thin as I sat in this room alone. I had too much shit to lose to get impatient and slip up. So I placed a fake smile on my face and braced myself for what was next.

~~~

I pulled into the parking structure of the strip club angry as fuck! Those mothafuckas had me sitting in that interrogation room for fucking hours. I threw the car into park and sat there for a moment and took a deep breath. *They have nothing, there is no way they can pin Honey's death on me,* I said to myself as I looked into the rearview mirror, checking my makeup.

Flipping up the mirror, I hopped out the car and made my way towards the entrance of the club. But before I could enter, the doorway was blocked by a petite, light-skinned woman who was dressed in an all-black jumpsuit with big sunglasses covering her eyes. She tapped her foot with her arms crossed, clearly irritated.

"Excuse me," I said as friendly as I could.

"Oh, I'm sorry, but excuse me ma'am. I'm having a little issue."

"Ok well, hopefully I can help you. My name is Na'Tya'. I'm the owner."

"Oh, so you're the owner"

"That's right, so how can I help you?"

"You can help by not fucking my husband!"

"Excuse me?"

"Bitch you heard me! Stop fucking my husband! You think I wasn't going to find out yo' tramp ass was fucking him!"

"Look bitch, I don't know what you talking 'bout, but what you need to do is calm your tone talking to me like that in front of my mothafuckin' establishment!"

"Oh, so you don't know that you was fucking Travis!"

As soon as she said Travis's name, I was shocked. I knew that he was married, but I never would have thought that his wife would come and confront me.

"Yeah bitch, don't look all surprised now! I'm only going to tell you this once: stay the fuck away from my husband! And if I find out that you still tiptoeing around him, I will make sure that Travis will be the last husband you ever fuck in your life!"

"Are you threatening me bitch!"

"Yes I am you fucking homewrecker."

I stood there and let out a little laugh. This bitch actually had the audacity to stand in my face and throw threats at me. I lunged at Travis's wife and grabbed her around her neck. I was going to choke the life out that hoe for disrespecting me. But for a small, petite woman, she was strong.

She started to scratch at my arms before grabbing ahold of my hands and prying them from around her neck. After she got my hands loose, she head-butted me in my nose, causing it to bleed. Filled with rage, I swung violently, making sure every punch connected with her face. We tussled about in front of the entrance, exchanging blows until she tripped up and fell onto the ground.

I dove on top of her and punched her repeatedly until my knuckles started to bleed. The club security guards filed out of the club, having heard all the commotion, and pulled me off the bitch. Travis's wife hopped up off the ground like she was ready for more, but the other security guard grabbed her before she got too close to me. But that didn't stop her from ranting and raving like a mad woman.

"You fucked with the wrong bitch! You fucked with the wrong woman's man, hoe! You'll regret the day you ever fucked with him you dirty ratchet slut!" She laughed hysterically while she spat a wad of spit and blood at me before getting escorted off the premises.

My blood boiled as one of my security guards escorted me upstairs. Bad enough I got issues with Honey and the investigators, now I got this crazy bitch on my hands.

If it wasn't so hot because of Honey's death, I would have killed that bitch and had Travis fix this shit. Instead, this bitch better be thanking her lucky stars that I'm allowing her to live to see another day.

Na'Tiva

A week had passed after my fatal encounter with the Reaper. I had stayed with Gunz for a whole week and now I was back home with 'Tya. As far as we knew, it was as if the Reaper fell off the face of the earth. But just in case, Gunz had one of his goons stay close and watch over me. I walked into the living room only to see 'Tya sitting on the couch taking a puff from her large blunt. That alone signaled that she was under stress.

"What's going on?" I asked as I sat next to her.

"Too much shit..." She exhaled her smoke.

"Shit, same here. Let me get some," I replied, causing her to look surprised.

"Well damn...what happened to the prissy little 'Tiva?" she asked as she passed me the blunt.

"Girl that shit is dead and gone. I'm on some other shit," I answered before taking a hit.

"Oh yeah, like what? Yo' ass been gone for a whole damn week and shit. What you been up to?" 'Tya interrogated.

"I been working on this deal with one of the biggest connects out here. I think this can take our business to the next level. Something that can generate us more money and power out here on the streets. I already know you got the escort biz goin' on, but this is different," I explained.

"How you know about the escort biz?" 'Tya asked, taken aback by my info.

"It wasn't hard to figure out when you had girls that weren't our strippers come in and have meetings with you in your office," I commented, causing a smile to cover her face.

"You smart-ass bitch!" She laughed and threw a toss pillow at me.

"You better believe it!" I joked.

"So what's this deal that you have with the connect?" she asked, getting back to business.

"The deal is to create an underground route at our club and move weight. We can have an exclusive group of clientele that would come to get their product and some entertainment. That way we can get paid on the front and back end," I explained.

"Hmm, that might not be bad. As long as we don't get caught up and can make more money, I'm with it." She shrugged.

"Good. I'm waiting on the connect's response on the deal and we can go from there."

"Aww shit! My sister 'Tiva is on some power moves shit!" 'Tya exclaimed.

"Shit, I'm trying to build an empire."

"Well I'm with you. Just let me know and we can get the basement hooked up and ready to move some work," 'Tya suggested.

"Ok." I nodded my head in agreement. Now that I got my sister on board, all I needed was word from Gunz about what the connect said about my offer and we could get this shit started.

By the time I heard back from Gunz, it was two weeks later. Luckily for me, the connect was with it. I would get 50 percent of the sales and Gunz would be my partner that I would have to work closely with. With those terms, who could say no to that? Just from knowing him in the past, I knew Gunz was a loyal nigga, so I didn't mind working with him closely. Plus, I would now have some allies when it came to taking Brandon's bitch ass down.

A smile covered my face when I got off the phone with Gunz. Now it was officially time to take shit to another level!

Chapter Six

Na'Tiva

Six months later

My six-inch, black-fringed Giuseppe Boots clicked against the cement steps as I made my way down to our underground warehouse. All eyes were on me as soon as I got to the bottom step. I stood there and scanned the entire floor level of my many workers doing what they were designated to do.

I felt a strong sense of pride staring out at our large warehouse full of large-scale work and heavy manpower. My whole life had changed as soon as Gunz called me and told me that the connect agreed to my offer to distribute his drugs from our club.

With the men constantly spilling out of my strip club, I was making a killing by starting an underground club where men could get ass and their drug of choice. Only top-tier clients were invited to our underground club at a private and separate location we opened up, while others had to get their drugs from my workers on the blocks. We never had issues with law enforcement since 'Tya had major connections to keep us covered. Everything was running smoothly, and we were making so much fuckin' money, I didn't even know what to do with all of it.

I was changing the game, taking over the "men's world of entertainment" and making it a "woman's game."

As I walked through the warehouse, observing each and every worker, they greeted me with a "Hey Boss" or "How you doin' Lady Hustla?" I had earned a name for myself. No one knew me as Na'Tiva from back in the hood, they knew me as Lady Hustla. I didn't even feel or look like the Na'Tiva that first came back to visit Akron. Even though I went through all the surgeries for my face, I opted to keep one long scar that ran across one side of my face. I wanted to keep something to remember the pain that I endured from loving the wrong nigga. Shit, now that I think about it, how many niggas have I loved that at one point fucked me over?

Every single one!

So as of now, I didn't have room for love. The only love I had was for the money, power, and respect. It was as if I got high off those three. They were my drugs and motivation to keep on living. A nigga could never do that for me anymore. I felt like the supreme bitch that reigned over the streets of Akron and was now taking over the state of Ohio. Gunz and I were doin' the damn thing, and didn't even trip about the competition. We were our own fucking competition.

After all the shit I been through to create this dynasty, I would be damned to let anyone ruin it.

"Wassup?" Gunz greeted as I approached him.

"Just checkin' in to see how everything is going. Gotta make sure shit runs smooth."

"I feel you. But you know we run a tight ship down here. Ain't nothin' to worry about ma'," Gunz reassured me.

"You got that right." I smiled. "How'd that drop go? The one to Ricardo out in Columbus?" I asked.

"Real good. They should be back in about thirty minutes ready to do another," he informed.

"Good." I nodded. "Well let me go upstairs and handle some business with the club."

"Aiight. Holla at me if you need me," Gunz replied before I made my way back up the stairs.

I had been so focused on our shit, I hadn't spent much time working with the main strip club's business activities. I normally let 'Tya and Monica handle that, but since things were going so good downstairs, I decided to go upstairs and get back in the mix.

Once I finally got settled at my desk, 'Tya busted into the office with anger covering her caramel face.

"What the fuck is wrong with you?" I asked.

"It's all fucked up!" she fumed. "All our events for this month got cancelled, half of our fuckin' strippers quit this week, and now our money is being unaccounted for. Our shit is all fucked up, and if the club gets hit then all our shit gets hit hard," she explained.

"Our money is being unaccounted for? You saying that someone is fuckin' stealing from us?" I snapped.

"That's what it is lookin' like. I gotta find out what the fuck is goin' on 'Tiva. We can't have this shit happen," she yelled in anger as she grabbed her purse and car keys.

"Aiight. While you do that I'mma have some of my niggas help find out who's behind this shit," I said before grabbing my phone and dialing up one of my accomplice's number. As she left, I made a quick call and told that nigga to find out who the fuck was behind swiping our girls and to get to the bottom of this shit.

Once 'Tya left my office, I couldn't help but flip out. In a fit of rage I knocked everything off the desk and let out a loud scream! "What the fuck!" was all I said over and over again. Just when things was going good for me, this bullshit happens. If business is bad, then that means no customers at the club, and if there are no customers, that means I can't push my work.

Damn! Just when I got that big shipment comin' in! I got to figure this shit out quick, because if I don't move this work in a month, that is my ass, and that is something I can't afford right now.

After calming down a little bit, I knelt down and started to pick up the things I knocked down. But before I could even gather anything up, my office phone started to ring.

I looked amongst all the scattered things on the floor before I saw the phone tipped over with the red button flashing. I quickly hopped up and grabbed the phone and answered it.

"Hello?"

"That was a nice stunt you pulled stabbing me in my eye 'Tiva."

"Reaper?"

"Don't sound so scarred 'Tiva. You thought you got rid of me didn't you?" he laughed.

"What do you want?"

"Well, it would be nice if you could give me back the money that you stole back in the day plus interest."

"You know good and well I can't pay you that back."

"Why not? You been stomping around town like you own the fucking place since you got that surgery."

"How the fuck you know about that?"

"No one can make a move in this city without me knowing. I even know about the little alliance you have with the people that those fuck niggas, Gunz and B-Moore, roll with."

"Then if you know that, why are you calling me? You trying to scare me or send me a threat?"

"This newfound attitude of yours is intriguing, and the fact that you running around here having people call you Lady Hustla is even more comical. Well, Lady Hustla, just a word of advice: you don't have to worry about me...at least not yet, since I'm not the only one gunning for your ass. So I'mma sit back and enjoy the show. But when I come for you and put that bullet in yo' head, it will be when you least expect it," he said before hanging up.

The dial tone buzzed in my ear before I hung up the phone. *What the fuck did he mean other people gunning for me?* I thought as the phone started to ring again in my hand.

"What the fuck do you want!" I screamed into the phone, thinking it was the Reaper.

"Damn Lady Hustla, you told me to call you when I got enough information about what happened to our girls," the deep voice of my henchman Rocko said.

"Shit, my bad Rocko. Tell me what's going on."

"There is a new strip club called Exotic Dynasty that's been recruiting our girls left and right."

"Exotic Dynasty? I never heard about that fucking strip club."

"Yeah, some nigga named Kyree from out of state just came and opened up shop. The word is that he got a better offer on the table that Flawless Entertainment can't even compete with," he explained.

"Are you fucking serious! I know we are competitors and all, but why the fuck is he taking my girls?"

"Cause there was a rat that linked all our information about the work, the girls, and how much we was banking nightly."

"Who the fucked ratted us out?"

"One of the dancers that was let go named Diva."

"That fucking bitch! We got to handle this quick, and when I say quick I mean right fucking now!" I demanded.

"Yes Lady Hustla. What do you need done?"

"Spray that whole fucking bitch! I don't want any survivors, you hear me! And make sure you don't get caught!"

"I'm on it," Rocko said before hanging up the phone.

I hung the phone up and thought about the new information that Rocko just told me. I couldn't believe that bitch Diva sold us out! To a competing club at that. We were the ones that brought her into this game, and I was going to be the one to take that bitch out! If these hoes in this club couldn't be loyal to the business, then they were dead to me.

~ ~ ~

"It's about to go down" was all Rocko texted me an hour before our plan was about to go into full effect. We had it all mapped out for this weekend. Him and the crew would go and spray up the Exotic Dynasty club while I went out of town. The last thing I needed was to be on the list for possible suspects since they were my new competition. We had this shit all mapped out. 'Tya was gonna handle business as usual, with the dancers we still had at our club. Gunz and the crew cleared out all our products and moved them over to another one of our locations, just in case shit went awry. And I was gonna go on my weekly trip as my alibi since that was normal for me.

Packing my final suitcase, I hopped in my all-black Maserati and headed to the airport. The cold winter air hit me as I walked through the parking lot and made my way to the entrance. All eyes were on me as I strutted through the Akron-Canton airport in my Russian sable fur coat and six-inch heels. I was used to all eyes being on me, but there was something about today that felt overbearing. Maybe I was just paranoid since tonight was when shit was supposed to go down.

I shrugged off my awkward feeling and continued to go through the normal routine at the TSA checkpoint.

As I finally approached the woman behind the small counter collecting our boarding passes, she barely made eye contact with me like she did with the other boarders.

She shot me a puzzled look after observing my plane ticket longer than normal.

"Is everything ok?" I asked.

"Just a moment ma'am." She smiled as she walked over to another woman behind the counter of the flight next to us.

I stood there in confusion as I watched them talk. Before I could make another move, police came out of nowhere and surrounded me.

"Put your hands up where I can see them!" An officer yelled out.

"What the fuck? What are you talking about?" I yelled in pure confusion as I held my hands up.

"You are under arrest for attempted murder, sex trafficking..." the officer spoke while going down the list of charges. He began to read me my Miranda rights as another officer handcuffed me.

"What the fuck...I'm fucking innocent! I want a lawyer!" I yelled out.

"Ma'am, you will be able to contact a lawyer once we get to the precinct..." the officer began, but the rest fell upon deaf ears when it hit me that I was really possibly going to jail. My blood instantly boiled. I was infuriated at the fact that I was getting arrested, and at a public airport like this, but even more that my plan had somehow backfired on me.

What the fuck? How the fuck did I get caught up in some shit like this? How did this shit point to me? was all I could think as they escorted me out of the airport and placed me in the backseat of the police car.

Epilogue

Na'Tiva

As I sat in the jail cell, my mind began to pace. How could I have gotten caught? I'm too slick and too smart...the only way I could get caught was if someone turned me in.

"You got a visitor," the officer yelled at me, interrupting my thoughts. I slowly got up and followed the guard as he led me to the visitation room.

As I sat behind the glass, my eyes focused on my sister Na'Tya. Instead of looking distressed like how I thought she would be, she had a different demeanor. Her long black hair flowed down her back, and her green eyes pierced me as she flashed me a mischievous smile.

"Having fun in there sis?" she asked. At that moment, I realized just who that somebody who turned me in was.... It was Na'Tya. My own flesh and blood turned on me and turned me in to the police.

"It was you bitch!" I yelled. She laughed.

"Oh don't be shocked honey. Back when you left me and mom in Akron so you could be a prissy little college bitch, who had to hold it down and take care of mom? Me! Who had to hustle and get shit done while you sat there with your nose all up in the air? Hmm...let me think, oh yeah, me! Then after your little man tried to bring you down, who helped show you the ropes? Me once again," she chuckled.

"You think you big and bad, but really you aren't shit but a dumb broad. I'm the master behind it all and you were just the puppet. You thought Diva was the competition, but if you used your head, you would know she wasn't that smart from jump. Who else could've swiped your girls and business under your nose? Only yours truly." She smiled proudly.

"You thought you was doing the damn thing with the connect. But I can't let you be out here taking over the streets." She laughed. My stomach churned with disgust as my blood boiled.

"Aww, don't be mad baby," she taunted as she stood up, grabbing her purse and belongings. "Remember honey, you said it yourself. It's a woman's game, and may the best woman win. Clearly it wasn't you," she said, leaving me in pure rage.

First B-Moore, then the Reaper, and now my own fuckin' sister? I had a whole list of niggas thewt I'm going to come after. I don't know how I'd make that happen, but one thing I knew for sure. When I get out this shit, I'mma make sure to skin that bitch alive!

I AM The Streets 3:

All hell breaks loose when Na'Tiva finds out her sister's dirty little secret. While Na'Tya is living the good life, reaping the benefits of Na'Tiva's hard work, she has no idea what her older sister and the mysterious connect will have in store for her.

**Find out what happens in part three of
I AM The Streets! Available Now!**